NOW WHAT?

An Appalachian View From Resume Speed, West Virginia Population: 2 Old People and 2 Cats

by James E. Martin

NOW WHAT?

Appalachian View from Resume Speed, West Virginia Population: 2 Old People and 2 Cats

By

James E. Martin

ISBN: 1-4033-9388-5 (e-book)
ISBN: 1-4033-9389-3 (Paperback)

This book is printed on acid free paper.

1stBooks - rev. 03/15/03

ACKNOWLEDGEMENTS

I am so greatly blessed to have the support and encouragement of my loving family which includes Betty, my high school Sweetheart and Wife of fifty six years; my Son, Rodney and his Wife, Sharon; my Daughter, Sue White and her Husband Jim White; and my two wonderful Granddaughters, Jessica and Jana White.

In addition to my Family, I would be remiss if I failed to thank my closest Friends who have laughed with me and tolerated me through so many years. Thus, my gratitude to Rex and Norma Sanford, Richard and Phyllis Blankenship, Robert and Sandra Martin, Norman and Katherine Roberts, Raleigh and Billie Sanford, Fred and Ann Bolt, and Harold and Beverly Frantz.

There is so much that I owe in love and appreciation to the Faculty and hundreds of Students at The White Sulphur Springs Elementary School, where I have served as a volunteer reader for several years. I am especially indebted to the following teachers for their friendship and encouragement: My Daughter, Sue White; Kay Napier; Debra Ramsey; Carol Polk; Shannon Moran; Lu Hefner; Debbie Alderman, Brenda Barry; Julie Gillilan; and Mikki Dixon. Special gratitude is given Principal. Pat Brackenrich for installing my 'Grandpa Ed's Bedtime Stories' and 'Ebbie's Newspaper Kite' children's books in the School Library.

I extend special recognition and thanks to the Librarians of Greenbrier, Monroe, Raleigh, and Jackson County Public Libraries, all of whom have enthusiastically accepted my previous books into their collections. They are: Phyllis Auvil of Alderson; Ann Farr and Christie Grimm of Lewisburg; Kimberly Spencer of Quinwood; Debra Lee Goddard and Geraldine Manspile of Rainelle; Valerie O'Brien of Ronceverte: Cherie Davis of Rupert; Mary Jane Walkup of White Sulphur Springs; Danny McMillion of Beckley; Cindy Laws of Peterstown; and Doris Weikle McCurdy of Union, and Edwin Rauh of Ripley.

I am also equally grateful for the valuable assistance afforded me by the Staff of the West Virginia Library Commission at Charleston; The Lewisburg Friends of The Library; and to The Ruitan Clubs of West Virginia including the Organizers and Volunteers of The Annual Ruitan Roundup.

I reserve special gratitude to my Friend and Author of the award-winning book 'The Well Ain't Dry Yet', Belinda Anderson of Asbury, West Virginia for her encouragement.

To all of my other friends including the memories of those deceased who have spent time with me, befriended me, have shared their stories, and have so greatly enriched my life, I also dedicate this book.

James E. Martin

INTRODUCTION

As a boy living on a farm atop Little Sewell Mountain seven miles Southeast of Rainelle in Western Greenbrier County, West Virginia beginning June 1929 when my Father bought our farm, entertainment consisted almost entirely of what One created for Himself. Those were difficult times just prior to The Great Depression. Rural life-styles were simple during that period of economic decline with the chances of survival by farm folk almost completely dependent upon the soil. Hard times yes, but not entirely unpleasant. My Family believed that what didn't kill you outright made you tough. We had no alternate choice. If One wished to survive, get on with living and time will take care of itself.

Much of my pleasure came from listening to the community's old folk telling stories, many of which were true, many exaggerated but told to be absolutely true. Lets say that some were enhanced a bit. Planting and harvesting by hand was hard labor, but it became much easier when neighbors helped neighbors. Thus we became good friends spending much time together. We walked from farm to farm to reach the work-site of the day and often visited each other during the early night time hours. It was always a treat for me when the story telling would begin. I would sit on the floor with my back resting against a wall and listen attentively to many wonderful tales.

I have always thought that for a person to be a good story teller, One has to also be a good listener. An old truism admonishes that One cannot learn anything while talking. The very fact that I am attempting to write an interesting book about the past is that I was encouraged to do so by my two children and my two granddaughters, all of whom were such good listeners when I told them bed-time stories during their childhoods.

When I visit modern Friends, I still enjoy exchanging stories. Many times, someone suggests that a book should be written to preserve them. It is with that in mind that I submit the following stories. Some are ones worn threadbare by the 'old-timers' of my youth and many relate to personal experiences of my eighty years of life including time spent during as well as subsequent to a career as a soldier. I hope you, the Reader, enjoy all of them.

ED MARTIN

CONTENTS

The Washing Machine 1
Resume Speed 5
Freedom Of Speech 7
Misconception 10
Family Feud 13
Gotcha! 14
You Don't Say! 17
Ghost Rider 19
Under The Big Top 20
Saturday Night Fracas 23
Couch Potato 25
A Small Point Of View 28
Oooh! That Hurts! 29
The Church Fly 32
The Missing Moocher 34
Deacons Beware 36
Family Matters 39
Do Unto Others 41
Don't Awaken The Dead 45
Cash Flow 48
Wasteful Americans 53
Horse Sense 55
Applied Education 58
Historical Precedent 59
Divine Intervention 61
Love Thy Neighbor 64
Heaven 66
Pot-Shot 68
Foreign Aid 70

Sign Language 72
Could The Honeymoon Be Over? 75
Fightin' John 77
I Repeat 80
Oops! 83
Partly Ain't Good Enough 84
Splitting Hair 88
The Coal Town Toilet 90
Uncommon Fraction 93
Wedded Bliss 94
The Feed Store 96
Some Days Are Like That 111
Gourmet Soup 115
Where's The Beef? 117
Old Lam 118
The Old House At The Crossroads 123
Rusty 126
Our One Room School 134
General Jack's First Night Out 137
Paths 152

THE WASHING MACHINE

Every book must have a beginning. Since this is about country stories, the first story should be about one of the most kind and lovable men of our country village. The Year was approximately 1936 when he was near middle-age. He owned a small general store and was also the Postmaster. His store was located at a three-way intersection of dirt roads. Since my Friend was such an affable person, his store was a favorite meeting place for stick whittlers, liars, knife traders, tobbaco chewers, and such. A few could be found there during most business days, but the happiest times were after the evening meal onward to ten o'clock at night. It was at those times that much laughter filled the air.

The scene was almost always the same. A corner near the front entrance contained the Post Office. It was partially separated from the remainder of the store by a tall cabinet containing a little window with bars and a front containing rows of individual brass letter boxes secured by inset combination locks. A row of counter-tops extended the length of the store on two sides with a four foot walkway behind each.

An assortment of merchandise filled shelves from the floor to the ceiling along the walls behind the sales counters. A coal-fired pot-bellied Burnside Stove sat upon four sturdy iron legs in the middle of the floor. A square metal box with sides eight inches high filled with ashes was conveniently placed near the stove as a receptacle for air-delivered tobacco juice. Two kerosene lamps, which produced dim yellowish light, dangled from chains fastened to the ceiling. A few straight-back wooden chairs to accommodate customers were scattered about. Nail kegs provided additional seats as well as platforms for several checker-boards, the colored squares of which were almost obliterated from many years of constant use.

There were fewer night-time visitors at the store during summer months when most of the farm patrons worked late hours in their fields. It was during winter months when there was not much to do on farms, there was a jovial gathering six nights per week. Although the Merchant, himself, lived on a small farm, he did little of an agricultural nature besides pasturing a milk cow and raising a small garden. It is easy to understand that most of his time was required to operate the store and Post Office. For that reason, he had no urge to be in a hurry.

He did not own a truck. It was customary for traveling salesmen to visit their own customers on a weekly basis, so all the store owner needed to do to order new supplies was to wait for salesmen to arrive. Since my Friend enjoyed a lively conversation and was so friendly, he was a joy to visit unless you were a salesman in a hurry with a schedule to keep. The Merchant dearly loved to tease the salesmen and to keep them guessing if they were going to get an order or not. For them, that was very frustrating. Being generous beyond belief, he seldom sent a salesman away empty handed.

This story is about a particular salesman. It was the era when Maytag Corporation began selling gasoline powered washing machines. Very few of any Brand had arrived in our Community. That salesman must have assumed that he had a very good prospect with this Merchant, so with very little formality, he launched hastily into his presentation. The Merchant allowed him to work himself into a goodly amount of lather when he suddenly cut him off in mid-sentence.

"Young man. Don't need one. Got one," he said.

Having assumed that he had no competition in that section of the State, the salesman was incredulous.

"Indeed, Sir, you you you have, Sir?" he stammered. "What Brand do you have?

"A Campbell," replied the Merchant with airy nonchalance.

"A Campbell!" exclaimed the salesman with disbelief. "Are you sure? I've never heard of a Campbell."

"Well, that's exactly what I've got," said the Merchant with a matter-of-fact manner.

"I'd certainly like to see it. Where is it?" asked the salesman.

"If you are all that determined to see it, you can walk to my house yonder on the hill, knock on the door, and my Wife will show it to you," replied the Merchant.

This story reached a sudden climax when the Merchant's Wife answered the door. The salesman introduced himself and said, "I sell washing machines. Your Husband said that you have a Campbell washing machine and I want to see it."

The Merchant's Wife, being accustomed to her Husband's practical jokes simply roared with laughter.

"Young man," she exclaimed. "You are looking at it! Did my Husband not explain that my name was Campbell before we were married?"

RESUME SPEED, WEST VIRGINIA

Have you seen those huge multi-million dollar estates with fancy portals and signs proclaiming the name of the estate? Well, my Wife and I reside upon a modest five acre plot bounded by Route US 60 near Caldwell, West Virginia. When we purchased the property more than twenty years ago, we made plans to make our place as neat and attractive as we could afford.

The entrance to our driveway does not have any fancy portals, but it was always in the back of my mind to make our place more than mundane. One day after we had lived here for several years, the Department of Highways established a forty five mile per hour speed limit through our community with the new speed zone beginning and ending at the corner of our vegetable garden.

The new speed zone inspired me to create a sign and give our property the name 'RESUME SPEED, WEST VIRGINIA POPULATION 2 OLD PEOPLE AND 2 CATS. Well, that sign does not make our place look like an estate, but it has generated much comment.

One day when our car needed service, which I scheduled with my Friend Bob at the Hart Run Exxon Station. By the time the car was upon the rack, two other of Bob's good Friends, Senator Robert Byrd and his Wife also arrived. The Senator was enroute to Lewisburg to dedicate a new medical clinic bearing his name.

Bob was having a busy morning. He introduced me to his two friends and had to take care of business. While waiting, Senator Byrd and his Wife talked to me for a while during which he asked me where I lived. In jest, I told him that I was the Mayor of the smallest town in West Virginia, but I doubted if he had ever heard of it.

That tweeked the Senator's curiosity. He said, "I think I know the location of every town in West Virginia. Quiz me. Where is it and what is the population?"

"It is Resume Speed, West Virginia, population 2 old people and 2 cats," I replied tongue-in-cheek. "It is a quarter mile west of here on Route US 60."

He was enjoying my joke when the Attendant who had serviced my car informed me that my car was ready to go. I paid my bill and was departing when the Senator asked, "Mr. Martin, is there anything which I can do for you in Washington?"

"Oh, I am so glad you asked," I replied. "I have been struggling with the Postal Department for years to get a Zip Code for my Resume Speed Post Office, but they won't cooperate. Perhaps you could help me,"

Obviously enjoying a good laugh, he said, "In Washington, I am known as the 'King Of Pork', but I don't think that even I can pull that one off."

FREEDOM OF SPEECH

During the late 1920s, a Traveling Salesman of some sort observed a young lad of our farming community alone hoeing corn in a road-side field. The lad was quite young, but due to his size, from a distance he appeared to be an adult. That young man was known to be somewhat retarded, was uneducated, and had very underdeveloped social graces. It is reasonable to assume that the Salesman was not going to miss any prospects for a sale, if he could avoid it.

The Salesman parked his vehicle beside the road. He immediately earned the young man's contempt by crossing a panel of woven wire field fence, causing it to sag. When he reached the location of the young farmer, the Salesman realized that he was not visiting a person who could make a buying decision. It has been said with considerable accuracy that West Virginians are very distrustful of strangers. That was very truly the attitude of that young lad.

Upon assuming his most presumptuous 'I am superior to you' patronizing demeanor, the Salesman said, "Young man, I want to speak to your Father."

"Wal, that's alright, I reckon," answered the Youth.

After scanning the entire field with his eyes, the Salesman said, "Well, I don't see him anywhere. Is he close by?" asked the Salesman.

7

"Yep," answered the young man of few words.

"Then, where in thunder is he?" demanded the Salesman with unshielded irritation creeping into his voice.

"Up yonder," replied the Youth gesturing indifferently with a thumb over one shoulder toward a low hill without turning his head in that direction.

The Salesman uttered something uncomplimentary under his breath and began plodding across the cornfield exposing his shined street shoes to the moist and sticky cultivated soil. With considerable difficulty, he climbed over a woven wire fence topped by a strand of barbed wire installed to discourage farm animals from reaching across to eat the corn when it later matured.

Both the fence and the cornfield now behind him, the Trespasser climbed the steep hillside in the hot morning sun. At the top of the hill, he encountered a similar wire fence surrounding a cemetery. He wandered about shouting, "Hello! Is anybody up here?" He continued to shout and looked over the far side of the hill, but after many minutes of futile searching without any response, he abandoned his search. Totally frustrated and mopping sweat from his brow, he returned to the cornfield where the Youth contentedly continued to hoe weeds and hill corn plants.

With undisguised contempt now, he confronted the Youth, "Are you sure your Father is up there?" he shouted.

"Yep," was the unemotional answer.

"Well tell me.   How long has he been up there?" demanded the Salesman.

"Wal les see," scratching his head as though by some miracle total recall would occur, the Youth continued, "Nigh onto ten years now ah reckon."

MISCONCEPTION

In the farming community where I grew to adulthood, there were 'tongue-wags' who would make jokes about neighbors whom the jokester thought were weird.

I knew the family about which this story was told. To lend some of my own observations which may support the opinion of the Originator of this yarn, I, too, considered the family to be peculiar. I hasten to rise to the defense of all who are peculiar. As a matter to consider, I, myself, may have been and perhaps continue to be peculiar.

During some of the direst days of The Great Depression of the 1930s, one of my neighbors who had a husky teen-aged son was approached by the Patriarch of the 'peculiar' family.

He said, "Neighbor, I see that you have already finished harvesting your hay. We have barely started ourn. We're way behind. We need help. Would you let me hire your youngun to help us? I'll pay him what he is worth."

My neighbor replied, "I'll have to ask him, but I expect that he will help you. What time do you want him to be there?"

"Just as soon after daybreak that he can get there, answered the old man.

That young lad was my friend and has remained so seventy years later. He told me that he didn't really want to work for the old man, but his Father insisted that it was the neighborly thing to do. He also told me that it was one of the hardest days work of his entire life. The work day began near daybreak and lasted until nine o'clock that night with one brief break for lunch and no supper break at all. For that day's work, the old man paid him one dime! The job was not complete, but my friend refused to return. A tribute to his Father's good judgment, he would also not permit him to return.

The miserly old man and his family lived at the end of a long private dead-end road at the canyon-like head of a deep hollow. According to relatives, the old man's wife in such isolation, starved for even the smallest scraps of news. The old-fashioned crank operated wall-mounted telephones serviced area during that era. First-hand witnesses reported that the old woman would dash to the telephone every time she heard other people's signal ring. She would eves-drop on their conversations. Reception by those early telephones was weak at best, so when an eves-dropper also came on line, conversations became inaudible. There were times when the old woman would break in and demand in a loud voice, "Will you talk louder and repeat that? I didn't hear it the first time!"

Now here is the part told by the jokester. He said that he met the 'Old Miser' along a country road one day. Addressing the old man, he said, "I heered yer dotter jest married a man twice her age."

Considering that the new Groom also resided with his elderly Mother and her equally ancient spinster Sister, the old man retorted in disgust, "Yep. She left two old people to go live with three old people!"

The Old Man also had another daughter and two sons living at the family home. The oldest son married a girl of delicate beauty from the neighborhood. Not only beautiful, the new bride was devoutly religious. As was often customary among farmer folk, the oldest son and his bride lived with the Groom's parents. Such was this case.

It is doubtful that the jokester was privy to any such conversation, but the following is his yarn:

At bedtime the first night of the new couple's marriage, the bride 'laid down the Law'. If her Husband was going to live with her, before getting to bed that night and every night thereafter, he would first have to kneel beside the bed and earnestly pray. Praying was a new experience for him.

When the newlyweds came into the kitchen for breakfast the following morning, the new Groom announced, "Father, I did something last night that I have never done before."

The new Bride hastily followed that enthusiastic announcement with, "Yes! And he is going to do it every night from now on!"

The old man responded, "Impossible!"

FAMILY FEUD

Haven't you heard that brotherly love does not always exist among brothers-in-law? Well, I suppose that is understandable, for after all, you do not have a choice when you acquire a brother-in-law. If you get lucky, rejoice! If you don't, it can be a 'bumer'.

This story is about two brothers-in-law who saw eye to eye only when they were sticking their fists into each others face. Both died during the decade of the 1920s. It made no matter how often they came into each other's presence, they would engage in a fist fight. One of them was a giant. The other, although not exactly small, was no match for the giant. The smaller one was tough, however, and always fought well, but the larger man always won. No matter how often the smaller man lost, he never quit trying to win.

Those fights even happened at family reunions and other gatherings much to the dismay of the two men's wives. Nothing noteworthy ever came of those silly events. No solutions. No compromise. No peace. Only a comment by the perennial winner, to wit: "Ah kin whoop im alright, but he won't stay whooped."

GOTCHA!

One of the most pleasant friendships I have had was that with my Wife's Uncle Joe. He was a real joy to be near. Perpetual good humor. Optimistic. Energetic. When I first met him, he was past the age when most people retire these days, but he carried a packed lunch and worked as a carpenter. He had many friends with whom he had worked for decades, but he had one loyal best friend most dear to him. He was a boyhood friend named Ig with whom he worked most of his adult life.

Ig and Uncle Joe lived a few miles apart in Charleston, West Virginia. They frequently spoke to each other by telephone at night, even after working together all day. They loved to play jokes on each other. Each must have lay awake at night thinking of new ways to play a practical joke upon the other.

My wife and I were sitting in Uncle Joe and Aunt Liza's living room one night when Uncle Joe lifted the telephone receiver, placed a folded handkerchief over the mouthpiece in order to disguise his voice, and dialed Ig's number. Ig had a habit of speaking rapidly; snapping the end of his syllablers off curtly. When Ig said "Hello", Uncle Joe used an assumed name and spoke as follows:

Trying to sound like the man on the six o'clock news, he asked, "Is this Mr. Ig M—?"

"Yes yes yes." answered Ig. "This is Ig M—speaking."

"Mr. M—, this is (Asumed name) from the Weekly Jackpot Program at WCHS Charleston Radio Station. This is your lucky night, because you have been chosen to answer this week's jackpot question. Are you ready?"

"Yes yes yes!", replied IG with anticipation. "I'm ready. I'm ready. I'm ready!

"Then listen very carefully. You get only one chance," continued Uncle Joe. "Can you tell me the name of Roy Roger's horse?"

"Yes yes yes!" answered Ig. "Trigger, Trigger, Trigger!"

"You are absolutely correct, Mr. M—!" responded Uncle Joe. "You have won this week's jackpot prize! Tomarrow you shall receive two free tickets to the Keerce Theater and one bushel of horse manure! Thank you and good night."

That incident was far from being either the first or the last in a long series of practical jokes. The following is another which I found amusing.

Urgent business caused Ig to make a trip by train to Cincinnatti, Ohio. He asked Uncle Joe to drive him to the Charleston Depot. Ig was dressed in a business suit and carried a small hand-bag. Ig purchased his ticket and Uncle Joe observed him insert the envelope into a side coat pocket. Uncle Joe created some small diverson which caused Ig to look away while Uncle Joe dropped a small piece of Limberger Cheese into Ig's pocket containing the ticket.

Within seconds, the train arrived and the two friends waved goodbye. As Ig described it later, he noticed a very unpleasant odor upon entering the car. He thought to himself, "They sure don't clean these cars very well." He chose a seat, but he noticed that other passengers near him arose and moved away. Ig thought that was a good idea for him too, so he left that car and moved to another. Upon arriving, he noticed that the odor was also inside that car. What was more, everywhere he went, people moved away. It was near one such moment when the Conductor entered shouting, "Have your tickets ready." It was also at that moment when Ig reached into his coat pocket and withdrew his hand holding a glob of Lindberger Cheese!

YOU DON'T SAY!

I have never felt at ease when attending a 'wake.' There is something about observing people consumed in sadness that causes me to feel incapable of doing or saying something profound or meaningful which would ease their pain. Many times I have wondered in advance what I could say which would express the depth of my sincerity. Most times, I merely say that I am sorry. I have observed others who also struggled to express their feelings.

Being 'old-fashioned' about proper decorum at wakes and funerals, I am disdainful of many attendees who treat such solemn events as though at a party engaging in loud talking, joking, and back slapping. My ability to abide by my own standards upon two occasions was severely challenged, however.

One night I was standing in line behind an elderly woman who was struggling to express her condolences to a bereaved gentleman. The woman was much taller than the man to whom she was speaking. In obvious desperation for some meaningful words of comfort, at arm's length, she firmly grasped one of the man's shoulders and blurted, "That old death will kill you!"

Upon the other occasion, my Wife and I sat upon a church bench to await the arrival of Friends who would also attend the 'wake' when a man and a woman sat upon the bench directly behind us. The woman, who obviously had a limited grasp of simple English, was attempting to read one of those little pamphlets containing information about the funeral plans which mortuaries make available. In a voice clearly audible to us, she came to the part which stated that the Deceased would be interred at a certain cemetery.

"The body will be int…int…" she stumbled. "How do you pronounce that word" she asked the man.

Obviously annoyed, I heard him snatch the pamphlet from her hand as he snapped, "Drat it woman! The word is enemaed!"

Having returned the tract to the woman, she reread the line, "The body will be enemaed at the Wallace Memorial Cemetery."

With the very thought of that scene, my Wife and I came 'unglued!"

GHOST RIDER

I live beside a major highway which skirts the bottom of a high mountain. A precipitous bank where dirt was removed from the base of the mountain in order to form the road-bed extends past my house in both directions.

A singing group to which I previously belonged met for two hours at a nearby town each Monday night. I rounded a sharp curve approximately one quarter mile from my residence one Monday night and saw a car which had rammed the high bank head-on. A police car with blue lights flashing was just arriving to investigate the accident as I approached.

I parked quickly and ran to the scene to see if I could be of assistance. I arrived just in time to see two policemen assist a greatly intoxicated man from behind the steering wheel. He was the only passenger.

Upon examining the driver to determine if he had any obvious injuries, the policemen realized that the man was 'soused.' One of the policemen said, "Mister, you are drunk!"

Limp as a noodle and with slurred speech, the driver said, "Yer absolutely right Constable, but I wasn't driving."

19

UNDER THE BIG TOP AT BUMPUS MILL

One morning during the summer of 1955, the First Sergeant and I, the Battery Clerk of B Battery, 675th Airborne Field Artillery Battalion, 11th Airborne Division, Fort Campbell, Kentucky, were at work in the Orderly Room. The First Sergeant, a bachelor, had a close friend, also unmarried, who was assigned to Battery B, 187th Airborne Artillery directly across the street from our Unit. The Friend had very large ears, so he was nicknamed 'Flaps,'

The tiny country village of Bumpus Mill, Tennessee lies at the western boundry of Fort Campbell approximately twenty miles from the Main Post area. The village was a favorite recreational area for many of the single men of the Fort.

On that morning, 'Flaps' rushed into our Orderly Room gleeful over the fun-filled evening he had spent the night before at Bumpus Mill.

Addressing the First Sergeant, he said, "Bill, you won't believe the fun I had last night! Talk about a blast! What are your plans for tonight? You've just got to to with me to Bumpus Mill."

"Hey, choke your motor and come back to Earth Ole Buddy," responded the First Sergeant. "What could be so exciting at that Podunk village of Bumpus Mill?

"Well, just let me tell you," prattled 'Flaps.' "Have you ever gone to a tent revival, Bill?"

"No I haven't," replied First Sergeant, "And I'll give you a clue; I am not interested in starting tonight."

"Aw, come on, Bill" insisted 'Flaps.' "I'm telling you, I've never had so much fun. Just let me tell you about it."

'Flaps spent the next half hour cajoling First Sergeant into going with him to Bumpus Mill.

"Ok! Ok!," responded First Sergeant. "It appears that the only way I'm ever going to get rid of you is to say I'll go. That is the only way I'll ever get rid of you. Now I have work to do. What time will we leave?"

"I'll pick you up right after evening chow," replied 'Flaps.' "I'm telling you Bill. You won't be sorry," he shouted over his shoulder as he went out of the door.

It was the First Sergeant's time to laugh when we arrived at the Orderly Room the following morning.

"I want to tell you, Martin, Ole 'Flaps' was right. That was the funniest thing I have ever seen," said First Sergeant. "I saw it and still can't believe it!"

By that time, he was laughing so convulsively he could barely talk. After he regained his composure, this is the story he told me:

Darkness was settling in when the two friends arrived at Bumpus Mill. The revival tent was located inside a hay field. A portable generator provided electricity to a half dozen drop cords containing bare light bulbs. The crowd was beginning to arrive and the Preacher was standing behind a pulpit welcoming people as they were seating themselves. Make-shift benches were made by placing two loose two by ten inch boards lain side by side atop short legged 'saw horses'.

'Flaps' entered ahead of First Sergeant and near midway he moved between a row of the improvised benches. Two people were already seated on the opposite end of the bench. First Sergeant and 'Flaps' had not looked down at the boards, but merely backed into the bench. Just as 'Flaps' was in the act of sitting down, a huge woman entered behind the two friends. She looked down and noticed the two boards were gapped apart several inches. In a milisecond, she clapped the boards together and plopped her great weight into a sitting position, thus trapping 'Flap's' 'unmentionables' between the boards!

In a voice of distress which could have been heard all of the way to Louisville, 'Flaps' was flailing his knees with both palms while shouting "Oh my God! Oh my God!"

Making the assumption that 'Flaps' had really gotten the Spirit, the Preacher extended his arms at a high angle pontiff-fashion and repeated over and over "Bless him Lord! Bless him Lord!"

SATURDAY NIGHT FRACUS

Witnesses said that the brawl was spectacular. It is hard for me to believe that many people in that 'do-nothing, lethargic, cantankerous town would unite in any cooperative effort, even to the extent of six men and one woman attempting to beat the stuffing out of each other. But, that is what the arresting officers said did happen. Three men teamed against three others. The woman was the 'girl-friend' of one of them. She influenced the outcome as best she could. Bottles, rocks, and knives were the weapons of choice.

Considering the quality of the citizens involved on either side, there is some doubt that it was fortunate the police arrived in sufficient time to break up the fight before the opposing sides totally eliminated each other. You know, one of those good riddance things.

At any rate, the usual 'looky-loo' crowd that always over packed the tiny Justice-Of-The-Peace court room to hear the 'juicy' details following such events were present at the trial. Each of the scruffy combatants testified about their participation in the fracus. Some of the men had received serious knife wounds, denture rearrangements, bumps, and scrapes.

At long last, the Justice questioned the woman. "Were you cut in the fracus?"

23

"No Sir," she answered. "Not right in my fracus, but about a half inch from it."

COUCH POTATO

A vastly over-weight middle-aged widow lived with her mentally retarded son in a small town where my new Bride and I also lived during the late 1940s. I was not acquainted with the widow, but I recognized her as a Patron of the Post Office where I was employed.

It is one of the World's social ills that, it you live in a small town for any length of time, you learn much sensitive information about the neighbors. That was especially true if one worked in a Post Office. The information truly was none of my business. Some of the 'morsels' can be very humorous, however. This story may or may not be true, although it was told to me by one of the town's policemen.

The widow did not have any visible means of support, but she owned her home, raised a vegetable garden, and seemed to be no poorer than most of her neighbors. Her neighbors complained to the police, however, that late on most nights, especially on week-ends, many people could be seen entering and leaving the widow's house after visits of only a few minutes duration. Rumors were circulated that the widow's only means of support was by selling whiskey during hours when the town's 'State Store' was closed.

The town only had a two-man police force, each man working twelve hour shifts. Being spread so thin, it was impractical for the police to mount a lengthy surveillance of the widow's house. When the neighbors clamored for police action from time to time, the night policeman with the assistance of a County Constable would periodically present the widow with a search warrant. The searches were always fruitless. The widow would 'keep her cool', just sit upon her sofa, and cordially invite the officers to come in. She would tell them to search her house if they must. Never finding any evidence, the officers would apologize for the intrusion and depart. She would simply smile, wave a friendly goodbye, and dismiss the intrusion without rancor.

Well, following one Saturday night of numerous complaints by irate neighbors about the noise and the traffic, the police with warrant in hand paid the widow a surprise Sunday Morning visit. As usual, the police heard the usual "Come in. The door is unlocked." The widow was sitting upon her couch as usual. Having searched the house without finding any evidence, the officers were voicing their usual apologies.

One said, "Well, as usual, we didn't find anything, so we will be going now."

Just at that moment, the retarded son asked, "Why don't you look inside the couch?"

"Yeah," responded one of the officers. "That's a good idea. Lady, please stand up."

The couch was the kind which could be pulled out to form a bed. The mattress had been removed to provide a rectangular storage box with sides six inches deep. The officers were amazed to discover rows of neatly stacked bottles of whiskey laying flat sides down.

Thus, the story ends. It is unknown if she ever got around to killing that kid, but can you imagine the damage it does to your community image to be seen leaving the house on a Sunday morning wearing hand cuffs?

A SMALL POINT OF VIEW

Children may be small, but they can usually make themselves heard. They are also the source of much of the most profound humor I have heard.

My Wife and I were visiting one of her relatives in Florida when our Host told me about one of her nieces who was five years old. The child's older athletic sister advised her that she should engage in some strength and endurance type sport early in life to avoid becoming a 'couch potato.' She followed the suggestion with the question, "Is there anything that you would like to do?"

The younger girl replied, "Yes there is. I would like to have a life-time membership in the church choir."

———— · ————

I have a tall and gaunt acquaintance who became totally balk at a young age. Although bald, he grew a magnificent full beard. He told me that he was inside a large shopping mall at Hampton, Virginia. He became startled when he felt a tug on one of his trouser legs. When he looked down, a tiny girl was looking up at him.

She said, "Hey Mister, do you know that you have your head on upside down?"

OOOH! THAT SMARTS

In the 1920s farming community where I lived as a child, very few automobiles traveled our dirt roads. We were still mostly reliant upon horses and wagons. I and most of our neighbors walked where we wished to go. Those who were more adventurous began buying primitive cars and trucks.

Tales were often told about farmers who bought cars after a life-time of driving horses; how they would crash through closed gates and other obstacles when wishing to stop because they yelled "whoa" instead of applying the brakes. Other stories described run-away teams of horses who became frightened by cars. One Ordnance in Charleston, West Virginia enacted in hopes of reducing run-away accidents required a person on foot to run a short distance ahead of an automobile entering the central business district shouting, "Warning! There's a car coming!"

Well, life was a bit more serene in our community as we made the transition into the 'automobile age.' There was a farm couple who lived a few miles from my home who bought a T-Model Ford. They were in the process of getting acquainted with their new toy by taking a short shopping trip into town on Saturdays.

Our bottomless dirt roads were maintained and scrapped smooth once per year. The surface did not remain smooth beyond the first heavy rain. They could be relied upon to have hub-deep ruts from end to end most of the time. Adjectives capable of describing their condition challenged one's imagination, especially during winter or following periods of heavy rain. Depending upon the width of the road-bed, one had the choice of two sets of ruts. Neither one was a better choice than the other.

Farmers' zig-zag split rail fences were frequently dismantled by motorists to fill ruts and, thus, get their cars unstuck. As you may suspect, the rails were never returned to the fence unless the wronged farmer removed them from the ruts himself. Most of the time, they were broken beyond use. Some farmers retaliated by removing the fence and allowed a hedge-row to grow in their place. A fair amount of money could be earned by keeping a team of horses harnessed and a log chain handy to pull stalled cars out of the mud. It has been told that some farmers kept the low spots adjacent to their property well watered during week-ends and holidays!

In the meantime, my friends with the new Model T were learning about the inefficiency of mechanical brakes. It seems that they were not doing well at all one Saturday at the top of a steep hill. The car gained amazing speed by the time it reached a sharp turn near the bottom of the grade. The front wheels tripped over a deep rut causing the driver to lose control. He was tossed out just as it upset over a sloping bank above a deep ravine on the passenger side with his poor wife remaining inside. The car slid on its side and came to rest at the foot of the bank.

The man ran half standing, half sliding down the bank to reach the car, which was not badly damaged. He scrambled to a position from which he could peer inside where his wife was frantically trying to free herself from dirt and weeds. Other than being disheveled and scratched, she was unharmed.

When he could speak, the man asked, "Are you alright Kumquat?"

"I think so," she answered. "But I think my danged neck is broke!"

THE CHURCH FLY

It always seems to me that some of the most amusing things happen at church.

When stationed with the US Army at Baumholder, Germany, my Family and I were seated in a chapel waiting to witness the wedding of a Warrant Officer's daughter to a young soldier. The Bride's father seldom wore civilian clothing, especially the tweed sport jacket and trousers that he wore upon that occasion. It must have taken great effort to fasten the jacket's single button, because he must have been twenty pounds too heavy to be wearing it. His trousers looked as though they would pop their seams at any second and their length was approximately four inches too short.

I had not realized that my friend was color-blind, but when the organist began playing 'Here Comes The Bride', I couldn't believe that he was wearing white tennis shoes and one bright green sock and one bright red one!

In another military setting while I was a member of the US Army Attache Office, American Embassy, Seoul, Korea, an Airman from the US Air Attache Office married a teacher from the American Dependent's Elementary School. The Airman's boss, the Air Attache, a handsome, single, flamboyant, wealthy Lieutenant Colonel pilot and his Korean chauffer arrived mere seconds before the ceremony was to begin. When the chauffer opened the car door, the Colonel, who was never seen in public without a huge cigar in his mouth, made long sweeping strides into the ante room where he hastily dunked his cigar into the urn containing the 'Holy Water!'

The title story, however, is about a man seated alone one Sunday morning inside a large metropolitan church. He was robust, but his most distinguishing features were an enormous aquiline banana-sized nose and his totally bald head.

The minister was early into his sermon when many members of the congregation were distracted by the bald man's audible snoring. If that were not funny enough, a pesky house fly was alternately making take-offs and landings on the man's bald head! The man, never-the-less, managed to concentrate on his deep slumber while taking occasional sub-conscious hand swipes at the fly.

All solemn constraints against out-right mirth were released when the observers watched the fly slowly stride across the man's head, down his forehead, down the bridge of his nose, and began to play hide and seek at the entrance of one of his cavernous nostrils! With the speed of light, the man in wild animation, clobbered the fly with teeth-shattering force with an open hand to his nose and shouted "Aw s—(expletive deleted)!"

THE MISSING MOOCHER

Who has not at some time been the target of a 'moocher?' They can be a real pest. A 'moocher' never seems to have anything of their own. "Give me a cigarette." "Give me a light." "Buy me a Coke." "Give me a beer." "Loan me a dollar." Just like Wimpy in the comic strip, "I'll gladly pay you tomorrow for a hamburger today," their demands never cease.

There was a soldier in one of my World War II Army units who was not only a 'moocher', he was also a losing gambler. Each payday just as soon as he drew his pay, he went directly to the Day Room where he would become involved in the first craps game he could find. Within minutes, he would go flat broke. He would even visit the local blood banks to sell his blood to earn enough money with which to gamble or to go on pass. As for his friends', they were subjected to his incessant mooching every day of the month.

The central character in this story, however, is about a lad who attended the same high-school which I did. He mooched everything from whomever he could. He was also adept at stealing other student's notes, copying their answers, and helping himself to desserts from unguarded lunch boxes. When observing other students leaving the school canteen munching candy bars, he used his great height approaching the unwary victim from behind, reach across a shoulder, snap off half of the candy bar, devour it, and go on his way.

A girl whom I knew decided that she would teach that 'moocher' a lesson he would not soon forget. She bought her usual candy bar, but she also brought two complete sticks of Exlax to school. She pretended to be holding candy, but was actually baiting him with the unwrapped Exlax. As usual, he made his usual pass. She allowed him to snatch all of the Exlax. As usual, he devoured all of it without looking at it.

Oh yes. The 'moocher' was absent from school for a week!

DEACONS BEWARE

I remember the first time that I saw that old church. It was a single story building with a tar-paper roof. It had a single entry door, two double-sash windows on each of its two longest sides, and all of its outside walls were covered by tar-paper roofing. It was supported by wooden posts rather than by a foundation. It was located atop a high sloping creek bank on a toe-shaped plot of land not much larger than the dimensions of the building itself. It was situated along an uninhabited stretch of a narrow country road miles from any other structure. It was shielded from a cattle pasture on three sides by a rickety field wire fence. Vast expanses of the cattle pasture was swamp land. Beginning at the ditch line of the road-bed opposite the church was a precipitous forest covered mountain at least two miles long.

Even at that early stage of my life during the late 1920s, I couldn't help but wonder why anyone would build a church in such an isolated area. Besides that, the building was cheap judged by any standard. At that time, it was obvious that the church was not in use. The grounds were unkempt and vandals had broken all of the windows.

I spent almost four years in the US Army during World War II and, upon my return, there have been numerous occasions when I passed that church. I married Betty Jean, my high school Sweetheart, during 1946. Her Father spent his entire life in that general region of West Virginia. The old church became a topic of discussion between us one day, so I asked him to tell me its history.

He told me that the church had been built and used by a primitive religious cult during the early 1900s and was pastored by an uneducated self-ordained minister. The meetings were typified by body-trembling trances, maniacal dancing, swooning, and rattlesnake handling. My Father-in-law was in his mid-sixties at the time of that conversation. He was a no-nonsense highly respected upstanding citizen who had fully repented a few youthful indiscretions of little importance. He said that he and some friends often rode horses several miles to observe what they considered to be frivolous but humorous antics by the church attendees.

Once when a week-long revival was in progress, at the end of each night's meeting, the preacher would announce the topic of the next night's sermon. He said that he would relate the story of Christ's Triumphant Entry To Jerusalem Riding A White Donkey. On the night of that sermon, my Father-in-law came prepared to test that preacher's faith. The preacher was proclaiming in a loud voice that he whole-heartedly welcomed the re-coming of Christ and that he would be the first to greet him if he walked through that front door that very moment! Taking that as a cue, my Father-in-law wrapped in a white sheet rode a white mule through the front door. The preacher was the first of many who dived head-first through the open windows!

During the mid-1970s, a new group of citizens, perhaps descendants of the original membership, experienced a new burst of enthusiasm for restoring the church. By that time, it was in a wretched state of disrepair. There were gaping holes in the roof, briers and elderberry bushes grew up through the holes in the floor and extended out through the four pane less windows and the doorway. A small tent was erected beside the church to serve as a temporary sanctuary and a place in which to have planning sessions.

At one such planning session, the newly appointed preacher was proclaiming to the faithful, "This sacred church shall rise again to new greatness! We shall repair the damage and we will cut the elders!"

With wisdom known only to her, but perhaps born of the social debauchery expanding in America during the 1960-70s, an elderly woman shouted, "Yes, and while you are at it, you'd better cut the Deacons, too!"

FAMILY MATTERS

When I was a child, my cousins and I would play a record on my Grandparents old gramophone titled 'I'm My Own Grandpa' The lyrics humorously described the singer's very complicated and probably incestuous ancestry. Without success, we would try to solve the puzzle of how he became his own grandpa. What I did not anticipate at that young age was that I would later witness a most intriguing family relationship which was similar to that described in that song.

There was a middle-aged man who would bring his family to shop at a small-town business where I was employed. He and his wife had several children among which was a seventeen year old daughter. As time passed, the man's wife died suddenly and, subsequently, his daughter married a young man who also had a teen-aged sister. The newly married daughter and her husband moved into her father's home with him and her siblings. Shortly after the daughter's wedding, her father married his son-in-law's sister. She, too, moved into the family home, so the brother and sister were both living in the same house once more. During the next three years, children were born to each couple.

Now, the older man had become his daughter's brother-in-law as well as also being her father. At the same time, he had become his son-in-law's brother-in-law. The daughter was not only her father's new children's half-sister, but also their aunt. Her father was not only her children's

39

grandfather, but also their uncle. The daughter's siblings were her children's aunts and uncles, but were also half-brothers and sisters to their father's new children. The father's new wife became her brother's sister-in-law and her brother's wife's daughter-in-law.

Now this dad-gummed situation has become too complicated for me to figure out. I don't want to spoil your fun. You will want to solve it for yourself, so GOOD LUCK!

DO UNTO OTHERS

It was near mid-point of my career with the United States Army when I met my good friend, Harry. He began his Army experience during the early days of World War II as an enlisted man, served during the Korean War, and was still on active duty throughout most of the war in Viet Nam. Following World War II, Harry was promoted from Master Sergeant to Warrant Officer. He was truly a great soldier, a credit to his Country, and a wonderful friend. We continue to stay in contact thirty four years since my military retirement.

You who have had the experience of moving your families from station to station throughout the World are aware of the difficulties finding suitable housing. I first confronted the problem with the outbreak of the Korean War when the Army was swiftly remobilizing. As was I, many thousands of men were recalled to fill the Army's needs for man-power. Also as myself, many had married following World War II and had families to care for. Production of domestic housing had all but stopped, and now, with remobilization, small towns near military bases were overwhelmed by the demand.

Many good people did their utmost to accommodate the hapless soldiers and their families by renting out apartments and spare rooms. Some saw the prospects for a good income by remodeling existing properties or by building small apartments. Many unscrupulous property owners converted back-yard chicken houses, stables, and woodsheds into shameful shacks for which they charged exorbitant rent.

In desperation to move my family from Charleston, West Virginia, I scanned the want ads and traversed the small town of Clarksville, Tennessee every night for weeks searching for a suitable place without success. I shall never forget one woman who showed me a converted chicken house for which she asked one hundred dollars per month plus utilities. She said that she dearly loved soldiers and had rented that house to many other GI families before. She related how she received letters from some of her former tenants every week telling her how much they loved her. The filthy condition of that place not-withstanding, a hostile rabbit could easily have kicked holes into the outside walls with hardly any effort at all.

As a last resort, I rented a small house which appeared to be structurally sound. I moved my family from Charleston during a week-end pass. We were overjoyed to be together again, but our joy quickly turned to disgust the very first night we attempted to sleep inside that house. The house was very old and all of the walls and ceilings were covered my multiple layers of wallpaper, much of which sagged, especially that of the ceilings. Being totally exhausted from the long trip after loading and unloading our furniture, we retired to bed shortly after dark. No sooner had we turned out the lights when we began to hear the widespread sound of hundreds of insects crawling behind the wallpaper. Alarmed that something might harm our son, I turned the lights on and discovered swarms of the largest roaches either of us had ever seen! They were carrying that place away. Fortunately for us, I found a more suitable place and moved out two days after our arrival and after detailed de-bugging our belongings upon the lawn.

One day, I told Harry about some of our housing experiences when he told me this story: He and his wife rented a two bedroom garage apartment from a man who lived in a nice brick house. In addition to the garage apartment, he had converted a shop building behind his house into duplex apartments. The furnished apartment which Harry rented was adequately clean and comfortable. The landlord explicitly warned Harry that he was forbidden to ever enter the garage. Harry did not see any problem with that. Except when the landlord was entering or leaving, the garage door was closed and locked.

Harry was required to pay all of his utility bills, which should have been meager, considering that only two people were using them and that he and his wife were away from home at work almost every day. When they received their electricity bill for the very first month, they were amazed. The amount was enormous. It remained exceptional the second month, then the third. Harry made his first complaint to the power company who confirmed that the meter reading was accurate. When Harry discussed the problem with the landlord, he said that the amount of electricity was not his concern.

The landlord's indifference caused Harry to conclude that something dishonest was taking place. He observed that neither of the duplex apartments nor the one he rented had power meters on the outside walls, but the entrance cables from each, including the landlord's house entered the garage building. Harry patiently waited for a time when he could observe the landlord leaving his garage. From a distance, he saw a single power meter located upon an inside wall. His suspicion was confirmed.

Without revealing his discovery, Harry asked the landlord if he would permit Harry to repaint the entire inside of the apartment if Harry bought the paint. The greedy landlord gladly accepted that offer and told Harry to proceed. Harry and his wife had located another apartment which would become available at the end of the month, and, since they would only have to move their clothing, they set Harry's plan in motion. They worked together every night to be ready to move when the time came to move; and when the time came to move, they did so without announcement to the landlord. They moved during the middle of the night.

Harry painted every room of the apartment alright. That is, he painted every wall, every ceiling, and every floor JET BLACK1!

DON'T AWAKEN THE DEAD

It was during the summer of 1963 that the Army's 82nd Airborne Division from Fort Bragg, North Carolina engaged in maneuvers against a Mountain Division from Colorado.

The plan for the maneuver was that the troops from Colorado were to represent an entrenched invasion force and the paratroopers were the liberating force. The maneuver area included many small towns and a vast agricultural region East and South of Greenville, South Carolina. Many poultry, dairy, and grain farms were located there. Pre-maneuver conferences attended by leaders of the opposing forces produced guide-lines of respect for and protection of personal and public property. The plans also called for the least possible interruption of normal commerce and activities.

Having allowed the Mountain troops to occupy their defensive positions, the airborne phase began with a coordinated troop and heavy equipment drop at six o'clock AM one sunny Sunday morning above the town of Joanna. Troops in the 'wave' with which I jumped landed on the west side of a highway while heavy equipment was dropping simultaneously along the eastern side.

I shall never forget seeing both a road-grader and a three quarter ton truck each having broken free of their parachutes, glide to earth in a 'skip-bomb' trajectory. The truck touched down just a few feet from a high chain-link fence surrounding a field flock of thousands of turkeys. The truck immediately burst into flames, crashed through the fence, and sped like a rocket through the field finally coming to rest at the opposite end of the enclosure amid hundreds of dead turkeys.

There always is much excitement during any mass parachute jump, as well as some irony. In a chance in a million, one young paratrooper, whose home was in Joanna, landed inside his own Mother's vegetable garden. He later told that, when his startled Mother rushed into her garden to see who had wiped out most of it, they were both surprised to see each other.

Another trooper landed atop a small house with a gable-style tin roof. He was saved from almost certain injury when his parachute was snagged by the structure's small brick chimney. He slid down the roof at high speed and off the edge of the front porch roof finally finding himself suspended between the roof and the porch floor. At that moment, the two residents, no doubt thinking that a bomb had struck their house, appeared in the front doorway in apparent shock. The friendly young trooper, with the aplomb of an Ambassador, voiced a cheery "Good Morning Folks!" As a postlude to that story, the trooper became acquainted with the couple during the span of the maneuvers and was invited back for diner a few times.

Well, the maneuver lasted approximately a month. Near its end, a highway bridge spanning the Saluda was the site of a rather brisk fire-fight, finally having been captured by the airborne troops. The Maneuver 'Umpires' assessed many casualties on both sides and had the 'Medics' attach tags of different colors to the uniforms of the casualties denoting the types of injuries sustained. Some had head wounds, broken bones, etc. A bright red tag indicated that the victim was dead. The Umpires separated the two Units and then moved on to evaluate other combat locations. The dead and wounded were told to remain where they were until ambulances arrived to transport them to field hospitals. Before the Umpires departed, they affixed signs at both ends of the bridge which announced, THIS BRIDGE HAS BEEN DESTROYED. DO NOT ENTER.

As all good soldiers do when told to wait, they all took advantage of the warm sunny afternoon by taking naps. As luck had it, the proverbial little old woman came driving her car. She read the sign and, not knowing what to make of it, she parked her car and came over to where the soldiers were sleeping. By chance, she chose a lad who was wearing a bright red tag.

She gently shook one of his arms and asked, "Sonny, does that sign mean what it says?"

Staring up at her, the soldier said, "You really shouldn't be talking to me Lady. I'm dead!"

CASH FLOW

Soon after the Meadow River Lumber Company of Rainelle, West Virginia ceased operations and began selling its assets, it also closed its Company Store and its Bank. Hundreds of men lost their jobs. Many who were past mid-life had worked there since their youth. Excepting those who lived in Company housing, the majority resided on family farms located in Greenbrier, Fayette, Nicholas, and Summers Counties.

One former employee whom I knew raised his family on his parent's farm, lived in their home, and cared for them until their deaths. Following their departure, his wife also died. His children moved away upon reaching adulthood, but their father continued living in the family homestead until his death.

Frugality defined the very lifelong existence of the man in this story. With garden, orchard, poultry, and farm animals for meat and dairy products, it was necessary to make only meager retail purchases. I can not remember ever seeing the man wear anything other than long sleeve blue denim shirts, bibbed overalls, a felt hat, and rough work shoes. As was the custom of most timber men of the era, both the felt hat and the overalls were put on new and were never cleaned or laundered. When completely worn out, each article was replaced by a new one.

The closing of the Company Bank presented a peculiar problem for our Subject. Due to his simple life-style and meager needs, he had faithfully saved a small fortune of approximately $40,000 during his working career. Forced to remove his deposit from the Company Bank, he sought a depository at another bank within the County, but he was treated with rudeness when he attempted to deposit his money in cash. Thoroughly disgusted, he responded by going to a restaurant where he obtained a large glass pickle jar. Living alone somewhat reclusively, he secretly stuffed all of his fortune into the pickle jar, dug a hole under the backside foundation of his barn, and buried it there.

I became aware of these events long afterwards, while managing my Brother's feed store at Rainelle. For ease of reference, I will call my acquaintance and some time Customer Gus. Now Gus had one real good friend whom I will call Claude. Claude was a frequent Customer at the feed store, coming in at least once each week. He had a pleasant personality and was interesting to listen to. He and Gus were involved in buying and selling cattle on a small scale and were involved in drinking whiskey on a much larger scale. Claude was more cosmopolitan in his outlook than Gus, his 'stick-in-the-mud' associate. That difference frequently caused some heated but harmless disagreements between the two old bachelors.

Some of their 'shenanigans' were especially humorous to me. Claude told me that he had to ford a shallow creek in order to arrive at his house. He and Gus seldom missed attending the Saturday livestock sale at Caldwell. He owned a three quarter ton pick-up truck upon which he had constructed a high cattle rack of rough mill-run inch by six inch boards. The truck's springs were much too lightweight and poorly suited for high center of gravity loads, especially lunging cattle. They stopped by the feed store on their way home. Rain had poured in monsoon proportions all day. Both had been drinking whiskey and were grousing at each other when they arrived. Claude had purchased a large cow and a larger bull which were crowded together inside the cattle rack. After buying some chewing tobacco, they departed.

One day the following week, Claude popped in and told me the rest of the story. There is a 'T-intersection' in a large down-hill curve where Claude had to make a left-hand turn into a side-road. The highway engineers had slanted the surface of the major highway curve away from that of the side-road creating what is called an 'off-camber' turn into the side road, That means that it caused the over-loaded truck to lean heavily to the right as Claude steered to the left. It was difficult enough for Claude in his condition to maintain control of the truck at that point, but he said that at that very moment, the bull decided to 'mount' the cow. The truck immediately rolled over upon its side spilling the two animals who escaped into a vast mountain forest!

With help from passing motorists, a wrecker was summoned and Claude's truck was reset upon its wheels. Darkness had arrived and the rain continued to pour. That Saturday saga was not quite over for Gus and Claude, however. A combination of poor visibility in the rain and fog, their overlooking the possibility that the water may be high in the creek, and their somewhat dulled perception due to their intake whiskey, Claude said that when they attempted to cross the ford of the creek leading to his house, they were sitting waist deep in water on the truck seat! The truck's engine wasn't running either.

Another day, Claude just came in to talk. He related that he and Gus were supposed to go to the stock sale the previous Saturday, but Gus was too busy and they had to cancel. He said that he arrived at Gus's house, but he wasn't to be seen. Gus never locked his house or any other of his buildings. Claude was accustomed to just walking in, so he did. Without being able to find Gus, Claude began searching for him at the barnyard. He eventually heard a noise behind the barn. That is where he found Gus with a shovel, rake, six foot long steel pry-bar, and a flash-light. He had dug a large hole beneath the foundation of the barn and was, himself covered with mud.

What had inspired Gus to do that was that he had by chance walked behind his barn and saw a groundhog burrow in the softened earth where Gus had buried the pickle jar! The groundhog followed the course of least resistance by taking advantage of the soft dirt. He had dug directly beneath the large pickle jar causing it to drop upon an exposed rock breaking it to bits. What the groundhog's intuition told him, but Gus did not know, was that there was a huge underground boulder beneath earthen barn floor.

Gus had retrieved hundreds of dollars which he could easily reach, but, when Claude aimed the flashlight beam into the finished groundhog tunnel, he observed a trail of greenbacks leading out of sight.

After giving Gus a thorough 'cussing out' for his stupidity, Claude's common sense prevailed. He simply bought a shop vacuum cleaner and attached an extended hose and was able to recover most of Gus's cash flow.

WASTEFUL AMERICANS

A US Army housing area at Augsburg, Germany is comprised of many multi-unit three-story apartment buildings, with the exterior walls of both the dining and living rooms containing windows which are both wide and tall. The buildings are flanked front and rear by concrete sidewalks.

My Family and I lived in a second-story apartment. From our dining room window, we could look down at a trash rack consisting of several fifty-five gallon open-topped drums. The Post Employees maintained the trash racks in a sanitary odor-free condition which did not elicit many complaints from the apartment dwellers. What most did have objection to, however, was some German citizens conducted scavenger raids on the trash racks on a daily basis. It was almost impossible to prevent them from doing that, because the housing area was open to the public, so the scavenger activity continued day and night. No one would object to the activity if it were not for the noise and the fact that the raiders would throw debris upon the ground in search of more valued items. Such litter became a real problem. The apartment dwellers became resentful of the practice. Some of the more mischievous children living on second and third floor levels resorted to filling paper shopping bags with water and water-bombing the scavengers from the window openings.

The windows tilted outward to accommodate cleaning. Although such design eased the ability of the housewife to keep them clean, to do so placed the person sitting upon the window sill in danger of falling. Many Germans enjoyed taking strolls along the wide level sidewalks, especially during evening times. Old men could often be seen walking slowly with their hands clasped behind their hips in a manner typical of leisurely strolling Europeans.

A story was told in jest that such an old German was strolling upon a back sidewalk approaching one of the trash racks. Before his arrival, an American housewife was said to have been washing an upstairs window, had lost her perch upon the windowsill, and had plummeted head-first into a trash barrel, thus becoming unconscious from the impact. Her feet and legs were protruding heavenward and her clothing was draping over the sides of the barrel. The old German stroller passed by, observed the woman's predicament, and commented, "Acht du Lieber! Those wasteful Americans! That woman was good for at least another ten years!"

HORSE SENSE

I reckon that on some Sundays, the Preacher is really that good. It was approximately five miles from an old man's residence to the church he attended each Sunday as long as he was physically able. He had faithfully attended that church since his youth.

I can remember that kindly old farmer very well. He never married, so he lived with his brother's family after his parents died. He seemed old to me the first time I saw him.

Now that I, too, am growing old and have become somewhat absent minded, it is easy for me to understand how someone can occasionally become befuddled. I do not relate this story in an uncomplimentary way, but rather to reveal the humor of it.

As usual, Uncle as he was called, saddled his horse and rode it to church. He was a bit late arriving, so the church yard was already crowded by carriages, autos, and other horses. He, therefore, lead his horse behind the church and tied it to a fence.

The meeting lasted until near noon, after which Uncle and the remainder of the congregation exited through the front door. Many of those in attendance had arrived on foot and returned home the same way. It seems that Uncle was so deeply engrossed in conversation with the walkers that he strolled along with them. He eventually arrived home where Sunday dinner awaited him. It was at the dining table that someone asked him where he had left his horse.

When living in the open countryside during 'The Great Depression', seeing people walking, riding horses, or riding wagons to their destinations was a common sight. One of our meal-time staples was corn bread. It was not only a staple during 'hard times', but we also ate it because it was good. Besides, corn bread was 'depression proof'; we didn't have to buy it; we raised the corn. My Uncle owned a 'grist mill' and we didn't have to pay him cash for grinding our corn meal, because he took a percentage of the corn as his fee. He didn't farm, so that was how he obtained the corn he needed to provide his family's bread, to feed his cow, hogs, and chickens. A good deal, huh?

Hand-shelling the corn was an 'all hands' family togetherness exercise each Friday night of the year. Since I was older than my brother, but too young to do much 'adult stuff', I was just right for saddling a horse, tying the sack of corn behind the saddle, and ride two miles to my Uncle's grist mill on Saturday. My Uncle was also the Postmaster and country store merchant. So, along with the shelled corn, I carried the chicken's weekly egg production, a few pounds of butter, and a few chickens to barter for our grocery needs written upon Mother's shopping list. I want to tell you, I dearly enjoyed that chore!

I often met others along the way who were on the same mission. I confess that I did not witness this; it was told to me by a friend. A peculiar old man of our neighborhood also carried his shelled corn to the mill on horseback.

When my friend observed him carrying the sack of shelled corn upon his shoulders while riding his horse, he asked, "Why are you carrying the load upon your shoulders?" The old man said, "I don't want to make my horse tired."

APPLIED EDUCATION

One morning during my military career, a Sergeant 'fell the troops out' for 'police call', an Army way of saying pick up litter and put it into the trash can.

I especially hated to pick up trash which someone else had thoughtlessly thrown down. I didn't smoke and I never littered. It was always difficult for me to accept why anyone would litter when it was certain that someone would have to retrieve it, quite possibly the person who threw it upon the ground. Da! It was tantamount to calling an artillery strike upon One's own fox hole.

I, of course, have attended many 'police calls', but I especially remember this one which I thought unique. While we troops were still at close order in three ranks, the Sergeant said, "Let me have a show of hands. All men who have a college education raise your hand and step forward." Several men stepped forward and formed a new rank.

The Sergeant then ordered all of those with a high school education to form a rank behind the college grads. With that completed, the Sergeant said, "Now men, all of these educated people are going to walk across this field and pick up all of the trash and the rest of you dumb skulls follow along and try to learn something!"

HISTORICAL PRECEDENT

My Wife and I leased and operated a Texaco service station located at the Hart Run I-64 and Route US 60 near White Sulphur Spring, West Virginia during the last half of the 1970s.

It was during that time when I met a kindly old gentleman, a Customer who was several years older than I. We much enjoyed each other's company. I especially appreciated his keen wit and wry sense of humor. I recall the first time I saw that tall gaunt man entering my place of business. I had images of Rip Van Winkle or Icabod Crane of childhood folklore.

I discovered that my new Friend was one of those old-fashioned mountaineers with a peculiar accent, sort of growling his words, but at the same time, voicing each word distinctly in unhurried precisely correct English usage. He also extended the ending of his words as though he were tasting them.

The old fellow died several years ago, but upon one occasion, he and I were confined inside the same hospital room for approximately one week. Following my release, a few weeks passed before he visited my station again. One sunny afternoon, he came in. We exchanged pleasantries and I inquired about what he had been doing. He pulled himself up to his full height with one hand resting upon my sales counter. He informed me that he had been back in a hospital located at Clifton Forge, Virginia. He stated that he was just returning home after returning to the hospital to pay for his treatment.

He removed a statement of account from his coat pocket and lay it atop the counter in such a manner that we both could read it. There were approximately thirty lines of itemized charges printed upon the statement which had been mailed to him.

With his growling voice, he said, "I may have made medical history this time, not that I have any objections, mind you. I told them if their statement was true, I did not object to paying the cost, because I would truly become world famous. So I direct your attention to line entry number seventeen."

My curiosity having been thoroughly tweaked, I read with great interest the line item to which he referred; a $79.00 charge for prenatal care!

DIVINE INTERVENTION

Just as were tens of thousands of other World War II veterans belonging to the 'ready reserves,' I was recalled to active duty with the Army when the Korean War started during 1950. I was assigned to the 11th Airborne Division, Fort Campbell, Kentucky. I moved my Wife and two year old Son to nearby Clarksville, Tennessee where we rented a small apartment.

It was at that time we purchased our first television. Two of the most popular prime-time nightly television shows during that era were Dragnet with detective Joe Friday and the DeSoto Motor Company sponsored 'You Bet Your Life' staring Groucho Marks. Our Son dearly loved both shows. Many times while playing, he could be heard singing the Dragnet theme song: 'Dum de dum dum…dum.' Groucho would end his show each night by admonishing listeners to "Be sure to visit your DeSoto Dealer, and, when you get there, tell em Groucho sent ya!"

After being stationed at Fort Campbell for a year, my Unit sent me on temporary duty to Fort Lee, Virginia for one week. Those were the days before Interstate highways, so it required two days of arduous travel each way by automobile. We assumed that my Parents, who resided on a mountain farm if Greebrier County West Virginia, would enjoy having their only Grandson visit them for a few days. We dropped him off while my Wife and I traveled onward to Fort Lee. That may not have been a good idea!

What my Wife and didn't know was a 'revival' meeting was being held each night at a tiny church near-by where my Father was a Deacon. As such, he and my Mother felt obligated to attend each night of the revival's duration. My Father also felt obligated to sit upon the front pew. As told to me by both of my irate Parents upon our return was the following story:

The Preacher was approximately five minutes into his sermon when our Son became fidgety. I can understand that a discourse about the wonders of fire and brimstone could be most boring to a young boy. My Parents became mortified when they began hearing the strains of "dum de dum dum" being sung by their Grandson! Many in the Congregation had difficulty stifling their amusement, which my Parents and the Preacher did not share. The 'final straw' broke my Father's composure when the Minister asked one of the elderly Breathern to dismiss the meeting with a prayer. The old man knelt upon the floor directly in front of my Parents and my Son who had become very 'antsy' and wanted to go home. Eventually, the man ended his prayer with "And when we die, in Heaven save us. Amen." At that instant, my Son sprang to his feet, faced the Congregation, and announced in a loud voice, "And when you get there, tell em Groucho sent ya!"

Prior to that time, I thought that I had been 'chewed out' by some world-class Masters of the art in the Army, but on that occasion, my Father proved me mistaken! I was only half way through his front door when he thundered, "Get that Kid outta my house! We'll never keep him again!"

His temperament got worse because of my uncontrollable laughter.

LOVE THY NEIGHBOR

One thing that all of our neighbors knew about Charity Emmalina Rebecca Bell Frantz Martin, my Grandma, was that she had no shortage of good moral qualities. She was as tough as rawhide when it came to self-reliance and determination. She truly cared for the welfare of her neighbors and was blessed with a generous heart.

This story is about a time when Grandma heard that one of her neighbors had the flu. She was about the same age as Grandma, but was already in poor health, the flu not withstanding. The neighbor and her husband lived at the foot of a steep mountain approximately two miles from where Grandma and Grandpa lived accessible by footpath through a dense forest. The woman's husband was ignorant and had never been overly endowed with ambition. In fact, he was generally considered to be a good-for-nothing 'moocher.'

My Grandpa was a hard-working old man who made his living in the timber business. He owned a sawmill, which at that time, was located twenty miles from his homestead. After commuting home after hard days at work, he ate most of his evening meals after dark during winter months.

A deep snow had lain upon the ground for several days and the word had reached Grandma that neighbor Ginny had not been able to cook for over a week and was in danger of dying from starvation. Grandma prepared a basket of food which was enough to last Ginny for at least two days. Granny could not make the trip through the forest herself, so she had the basket of food ready for Grandpa to take to Ginny after eating his supper. With the basked held in one hand and a kerosene lantern in the other, the old man braved the winter night to deliver the food to Ginny. When he reached the neighbor's house following the difficult trek, he knocked upon the front door. He had no respect for Ginny's husband and wasn't disposed to socialize with the old 'geezer.' When Ginny's husband opened the door, Grandpa asked how she was.

He responded in the weird sing-song accents of which he was accustomed to expressing himself, "I gosh, my woman mate Ginny is terrible poorly with th grip. Mighty poorly. Won't ya come inta th house an sit a spell?"

"No, thank you," replied Grandpa. "I'd best be going back. It's hard walking, you know. Uphill all of the way. Charity is worried about Ginny. She heard that Ginny isn't well enough to cook, so she had me bring her this basket of food."

The greedy old man's eyes bulged at the sight of fried chicken and all the trimmings when he took the basket and yanked back the towel with which Grandma had covered the contents.

He exclaimed enthusiastically, "I gosh, that there is too much for Ginny. Ah'll gest eat it myself!"

HEAVEN

One aftermath of my military career, part of which was in World War II and over half of which was spent as a paratrooper, was the necessity for shoulder surgery performed at Walter Reed Army Hospital, Washington, D.C.

I went to physical therapy at 10;00 AM and 2:PM each of the nine days of convalescence. On the second afternoon, I was assigned a permanent therapist for the remainder of my stay. She was the prettiest female soldier whom I had ever seen. She also had a last name which I have never seen before or since. Her last name was Heaven!

It was the requirement of my therapy that I had to be in close proximity to Heaven for two hours each day. Not what I considered hard duty at all.

Perhaps in consideration of my rank, I was accorded a well-appointed and comfortable private room. On the evening following my first meeting with Heaven, I was watching television inside my room when a Lieutenant Colonel wearing Chaplain's insignia on his uniform appeared in my doorway.

"How are you feeling tonight?" he inquired.

Without elaborating, I simply answered, "Ah Chaplain, I have never felt so close to Heaven as I have today."

The Chaplain beamed with approval. He responded by saying, "Bless you my Son."

POT-SHOT

One sunny summer afternoon, my Wife and I were attending a girl's softball game. We were sitting on bleacher seats when we heard an elderly lady on the seat behind us telling two other women about a shopping trip which she had taken to Beckley, West Virginia the previous afternoon.

She said that she was on her way home when she remembered an item she needed and had failed to buy. As luck had it, she observed a Wal-Mart store near by, so she hurriedly parked and entered the store. That is when she observed another elderly woman sitting on the driver's side of a car in the torrid sunshine with the windows up and the motor not running. She noted that the woman was slightly bent over the steering wheel with both hands clasped behind her head. The woman rushing into the store thought it was strange that anyone would be sitting in a hot car with the windows rolled up, but she went on her way.

Approximately five minutes later, the lady came out of the store and saw the other woman still sitting in the same position. Becoming alarmed, she rushed to the other woman's car to inquire if she was alright. Without moving other than to shout, the woman inside the car pleaded, "Call the Police. I've been shot!"

While the shopping lady used a telephone, the one inside the car remained motionless. Emergency personnel arrived within moments. A policeman approached the car and asked, "Can you open your door?"

The woman in the car shouted, "I can't. I have been shot and I am holding my brains to keep them from falling out!"

Thereupon, the policeman opened the car door. He did not see any blood, so he asked, "Are you sure that you have been shot?"

"Yes," the woman replied. I have been shot in the back of my head and my brains are coming out."

Totally baffled, the policeman opened the back door and observed a huge glob of white goo oozing from between the woman's fingers, but no blood. He asked, "Do you think that you can get out of your car?"

The woman said that she thought she could if she was careful, for she could feel no pain. That was when the emergency personnel discovered a large wad of biscuit dough smeared into the woman's hair!

Investigation disclosed that the woman had been grocery shopping an hour or so before arriving at Wal-Mart and had left the loaded bags upon her back seat inside the hot car with the windows up while she did some more shopping. When she reentered the car and slammed the door, the vibration was enough to cause a can of biscuit dough resting atop groceries in one of the bags to explode forcefully launching the contents with a loud pop to the back of the woman's head.

James E. Martin

FOREIGN AID

If you have visited Rome, no doubt you remember the huge and very magnificent Victor Emanuel Tomb honoring Italy's last King. In addition to the many steps leading up the front of the monument, I recall the swirling traffic both human and vehicular teeming before it upon the paved plaza measuring hundreds of feet both wide and deep. The process of getting from point A to point B at that site truly defines 'difficulty', most especially if one is on foot. While trying to approach the monument safely while also escorting my Wife and our two small children caused terms such as life expectancy, will and testament, traction, and convalescence to race through my mind. Also, I do not even know the Italian word for hospital!

Besides the zooming, honking vehicles which enveloped us on all sides and totally ignored the sanctuary of cross-walks and walking lanes, we were confronted by clusters of street venders trying to sell rosaries filled with 'holy water blessed by the Pope', picture post cards, trinkets, and jewelry. Since that 'no man's land' was those venders daily environment, they seemed oblivious to the danger that they were in and the danger that they were forcing upon the harried tourists.

Have you heard the phrase 'non-essential workers go home'? Well, to add to the confusion without rendering a modicum of difference to the maddening condition, the city's traffic control policemen could just as well have stayed at home. They were beautifully dressed in snow-white uniforms which also included a white helmet. Each one stood upon a small metal stand approximately two feet high. They all seemed to be programmed exactly the same. If it were not for observing their constantly and meaningless waving of their arms, their expressionless faces would lead one to think that they were asleep. They appeared to be pantomiming the hours away until their shift was over. The traffic completely ignored them and played the Russian roulette game of each man for himself.

I am still alive today, having survived the experience. Sometime later back at my Military Unit in Germany, a young Private First Class whom I knew also returned from a visit to Rome. He, too, had encountered a 'holy-water' street vendor in a stifling mass of humanity striving to avoid being killed by traffic in front of Victor Emanuel's Tomb. My friend said that he had never seen the man before and tried to ignore the vendor who was tugging on one of his arms and holding a water-filled rosary up to his face.

My friend said, "I can't buy the rosary. I don't have any money."

Upon hearing that, the vendor replied in 'pigeon English, "Do no worry Joe, Ima gonna giva you credit!"

James E. Martin

SIGN LANGUAGE

Signs really intrigue me. I am old enough to remember when there were very few signs compared to the blizzard of signs today competing for attention. That was especially true before development of our network of trans-continental highways and detailed road maps. Before the standardization of road signs and the vast amount of information which they furnish today's Travelers at a glance, motorists during my youth had to rely upon verbal directions given by someone who didn't know which Planet he was on, much less having the ability to direct a poor lost Traveler to a positive destination.

It is my conclusion that signs are the absolute shortest of all short stories. Well planned signs relate a complete thought with as few as one or two words. Their succinctness is essential for economy of space and, if their message is to be grasped by Motorists whizzing past at seventy miles per hour, they must be brief.

Being a child of the horse and buggy days, I enjoy the signs which I can read at a more leisurely pace. Many of them amuse me such as one located in a small northern West Virginia town which seemed to still be partially locked into the horse and buggy days during the 1950s. I have no doubt that the sign's message had been tampered with by some Prankster and that in its original format may have announced "BRIDLES REPAIRED", but what I saw was "BRIDES REPAIRED"

Having many teachers who insisted upon clear expressions of thoughts both vocal and written during the years of my education, I am often amused by some of the signs which school officials create. One in particular which is issued on an annual basis by our State Board Of Education when the school season begins each fall appears in the form of a 'bumper sticker'. It is a contraction which announces 'SCHOOL'S OPEN'. Any fourth grade Student can tell you that school's is possessive meaning that something belongs to a school, thus making the sign meaningless. If the sign is to caution motorists to be careful, why not state it correctly by announcing that schools are open, or if the apostrophe is intended to state that school is open, simply use the word is and say school is open?

I read an article in a newspaper many years ago which poked fun at teachers. It referred to a sign posted upon a door leading into a school cafeteria. The sign stated: SHIRTS AND SOCKS ARE REQUIRED TO EAT IN THE CAFETERIA. Some observant Student who saw the humor in the sign's confusing message used a felt-tip pen to add the additional message: SMELLY SNEAKERS CAN EAT ANY PLACE THEY WISH.

Have you ever pondered the incongruity of a sign occasionally seen upon a door which commands KEEP THIS DOOR CLOSED AT ALL TIMES? Duh! Why was the door put there in the first place?

Until approximately twenty years ago, there was a Greyhound Bus Station located in a small town near where I live. Just as did most bus stations, this one contained a restaurant named The Terminal Restaurant. The seedy appearance of the restaurant and state of cleanliness was not very confidence inspiring, especially when Travelers could look at a large mortuary located directly across the street!

Once I was stopped by a red light at a three-way intersection in Roanoke, Virginia when I observed a restaurant directly across the street which had been partially destroyed by fire. The restaurant's business sign, which had not been damaged by the fire, announced: EXOCTIC COOKING! My destination was located only a few doors from that restaurant. Upon dismounting from my car, I noted with interest a sign on the adjacent property cautioning: NO PARKING ALOUD.

I was especially bemused by two signs at a street corner in Orlando, Florida. The street sign under which I was standing stated that the street was DEAD END. I was also standing beside a building a few feet away at that corner whose window sign advertised ARTIFICIAL LIMBS.

It would be easy to write about dozens more, but the most outstanding of all was told to me by my Brother-in-law who was repairing a parking lot belonging to a funeral home in a town near Greenville, South Carolina. A sign attached to the front door bore the cheery announcement: WALK-INS WELCOME!

COULD THE HONEYMOON BE OVER?

Three weeks before I retired from the United States Army, my Unit stationed at the Federal Building in Pittsburgh, Pennsylvania sent me on a two week temporary duty assignment to Fort Knox, Kentucky. My Commander had made a one-night reservation for me at a hotel in Louisville, where three other colleagues from Fort Meade, Maryland were to meet me Monday morning with a sedan. I made the brief flight to Louisville on a Sunday afternoon flight and checked in to my room.

Near six o'clock Monday morning, I began a search for a restaurant to eat breakfast. After walking a couple of blocks, I found a Walgreen Drug Store which had a short-order counter with a dozen bar-stools. Being alone and not wishing to separate groups who might come in I occupied a stool at one end of the row. Soon after placing my order, other people began crowding into the store among whom were three attractively dressed young women. The Subject of this story occupied the seat next to me.

The two short-order cooks behind the counter became busy rather quickly. The one who came to take the young ladies' orders recognized the two girls farthest from me and merely asked, "The same as usual?" They both said, "Yes." He quickly started their orders and returned to the third girl.

He asked, "What will yours be Babe?" followed by, "You're new here aren't you?"

With the absolute broadest 'southern drawl' I have ever heard, she said. "Wal yes Ah ayme. Ah want bacon and a fried ayaig sunny side up or dowyn, Ah don know which. Ah really do want it sunny side up, but Ah don know iffin Ah can staynd that there yeller eye starin at me this tyme of tha morning."

"You're confusing me Babe," fumed the cook. "Do you want it up or down?"

"Oh fiddle!" answered the girl. "Jest scramble it."

While the cook prepared their orders, the girl-talk continued. The up or down girl said, "Ya know, this is the first time that Ah have ate breakfast out since Honey and Aye got married a year ago. I always fix Honey's breakfast the first thing in the morning afore he goes to work, but this morning Ah overslept. Honey woke me up. Ah didn't even know that he was shaved, showered, and fully dressed until he bent over me and gave me a kiss and said, "Good-bye Babe." And Ah jest flew outta that bed. Ah said, "Honey wait! Ah haven't fixed your breakfast yet." Honey said, "Yes I know Babe. There is something I have been meaning to tell you for a year; I never eat breakfast."

FIGHTIN' JOHN

During the mid-1920s, my Grandfather owned and operated a sawmill in the mountains of Greenbrier County, West Virginia. At that time, he employed at least two dozen men, some of which worked on the mill, others drove logging teams, cut timber, and one cooked at the bunk-house kitchen.

None of those men had graduated from 'charm schools' or had ever heard of Dale Carnegie's course of 'How To Win Friends And Influence People.' They were good at what they did, however, but at times, they felt misunderstood and unappreciated.

A case in point involved a little man who was approximately five feet four inches tall, weighing near one hundred twenty five pounds. He drove a team of horses into the forest to drag the logs to the mill. He had an incurable 'little man complex' although more stalwart practitioners in the art of attitude adjustment had plied their skills toward correcting his problem without measurable success. He was a slow learner.

Another person with an adversarial attitude was the two hundred thirty pound six foot four camp cook. Frustration over voiced evaluation and under-appreciation of his culinary creations always simmered either on or near the surface of his point of ignition. Like many temperamental 'artists', he had a few pet irritants which caused him to 'blast off' shortly after ignition. Since he was both cook and dishwasher, one of his most volatile 'pet peeves' was men eating desserts from coffee cups instead of from bowls. Gooey dessert residues were difficult to wash from cups adding to more effort to clean them.

Cookie and the little guy were, it seemed, natural born advisaries. They did not try to hide their contempt for each other. The storm was brewing over time, so it reached critical mass one night at supper. It was nothing earth-shaking; amusing more than anything else. With Cookie watching a few feet away, Little Guy dumped a large wedge of cherry cobbler into his coffee cup and leered at Cookie with a taunting grin. That really 'tore it'!

Cookie reached across the dining table and grasped Little Guy by the front of his bibbed overalls and yanked him into the air as though he were a rag doll. He held the little runt at arms length and growling like a bull dog.

Little Guy shouted, "Now you are in big trouble! You have tangled with Fightin John from Rocky Holler! Ah kin whup any man; put me in a rock pile and I ken whup six!"

All the while, Little Guy was taking wild 'hay-maker' swings at Cookie's chin without being able to reach it. His other arm and both legs were flailing in the air without touching anything. Finally, in a rage of disgust, Cookie flung Little Guy through the air where he landed on his backside in a dimly lighted corner of the room. As Cookie stomped back into his kitchen, Little Guy jumped to his feet and shouted, "Now, let this be a warning to the rest of ya,

Ya don't want to tangle with Fightin Jon from Rocky Holler!"

"I REPEAT, BACK UP"

During one of my assignments in Germany, I was a member of a small Detachment belonging to the 11th Airborne Division. The Division was preparing to return to Its home bases located in Augsburg and Munich following a month-long maneuver in a mountainous area northwest of Ulm.

On such occasions, all roads leading from the maneuver area were clogged by slow-moving convoys comprised of many types of vehicles large and small. Vehicles assigned to our Detachment were one two and a half ton truck with trailer, one three quarter ton truck with trailer, and eight jeeps with trailers. We were assigned a departure time of nine o'clock AM.

Our Detachment was commanded by a Major who fancied himself as an expert map reader. We members of the Unit were very familiar with the 'Major goof-up' which was about to happen, because we had witnessed similar events before. The Major summoned all of we men to gather around his jeep where he had spread a topographical map upon the vehicle's hood.

In vintage 'Barney Fife style', he announced, "Now Men, I have detected an alternative route on this map where no other Units will be traveling, therefore, we shall avoid all of the highway congestion. All drivers stay closed up so you won't become lost and we will get home far ahead of the Division."

That having been said, he gave the order to mount and move out. Each member of the Detachment were adept at map interpretation, so we could plainly see that the initial route that he had selected was indicated by a broken line meaning that it was a minor unimproved dirt trail passing through a major forest. Some of the senior sergeants as well as the Executive Officer {a Captain} told him that he was making a mistake. The Major, who was very contemptuous of 'subordinates' ignored their remarks and proceeded as he had planned.

The convoy was formed by the Major's jeep in the lead position followed by the trucks, then the remaining jeeps with the Captain in the last position. The convoy had to creep along much more slowly over the dirt trail than it would have if it had joined the remainder of the Division and had we taken our assigned places upon the paved highways. Disaster was not long in coming. Within a few miles, the trail led up a very steep narrow ridge such as hikers describe as a 'hog back'. Upon reaching its summit, we were appalled to discover that we were perched on the upper edge of a huge rock quarry which was at least one hundred yards deep! What was worse, if anything could be, that was where that branch of the trail ended!

Until that time, the field radios had been silent. The Major's driver was a Private First Class who held the Major's lack of common sense in contempt. When the Major realized the dilemma facing him, he ordered this driver to instruct all drivers to back up.

As if to show his disgust with the Major, his driver spoke into the microphone in a barely audible laconic manner, "Back up. I repeat, back up. I repeat, back up. I repeat, back up."

Distinctly audible in the background, the Major could be heard shouting at his driver, "Knock that off and shut up!"

Well, I ask you, have you ever experienced the difficulty of backing a jeep and a loaded trailer, even under ideal conditions? If you consider that to be difficult, can you imagine the task of backing a fully loaded 'deuce and half' with trailer a few hundred yards with hardly any wiggle room on ether side and the edge of a precipitous drop within a few inches of its wheels? Score one round for stupidity!

This story ended near midnight when we finally reached Augsburg after retracing our tracks back to our original morning departure point, driving out to a paved highway which lead to the Autobahn, and thus becoming the last Unit of the Division to get home. CHEERS!

OOPS!

A car salesman friend of mine told me this story about a fellow car salesman who frequently made 'boo-boos' when speaking. Sometimes the results were very amusing, but there were times when it was embarrassing.

A young woman called one afternoon for an appointment to visit the salesman the following morning at ten o'clock to discuss trading an ancient German 'VW' for a larger and newer car. Several people were present in the salesroom when the salesman, through a window, saw his prospective customer dismounting from her car. Just at that very moment, the salesman was called to answer a telephone call. To alert the other salesmen that the young woman was his prospect and to ask someone to greet her until he had completed the telephone conversation, he shouted, "Someone talk to that young lady coming in. She has a little 'VD' she wants to get rid of."

PARTLY AIN'T GOOD

A widow woman who lived near my childhood home advertised by word of mouth that she wanted to buy a cow due to birth a calf during early spring. Also living in the general vicinity was a devious old rascal who had the reputation of being ethically challenged. There never were rumors that he actually stole anything, but his truthfulness was frequently questioned. He was a cunning 'Old Cuss' who was adept at 'splitting hairs' and loved to make unwritten agreements which would evolve into 'you said, I said' confrontations whose outcomes were always slanted to his benefit and his adversary would lose his shirt.

That man watched the delinquent tax reports in our County's newspapers. He would target large boundaries of abandoned farms, surreptitiously paying the delinquent taxes for a ten year period, thus bypassing the possible claims of absentee descendants, and thereby acquire free land. Almost without exception, fences worthy of containing farm animals were nonexistent. Also, abandoned agricultural land in our mountainous area neither mowed or tilled began returning to forest after a few years rendering it unsuitable for pasture. The old man who was a 'horse trader' was notorious for releasing herds of both horses and cattle upon his fenceless farms. The results were that the starving animals free-loaded upon his neighbor's pastures, lawns, and gardens. Angry appeals to him fell upon indifferent ears.

Can you imagine your astonishment if you awakened one summer night to discover a horse standing blithely with its head protruding through your bed-room window? It happened to my Brother! His estate had a beautifully landscaped lawn which was fenced only on the back side to prevent his own farm animals entering it from adjacent fields. The front of the lawn was bounded by a rural highway. Summer nights were seldom extremely warm at his high mountain home, so bedrooms were kept comfortably cool by fresh air flowing through open windows. My Brother and his Wife were rudely awakened from deep sleep by a horse nudging them with its nose!

Needless to say, my Brother was enraged. He was further amazed upon exiting his house to find four additional horses grazing upon his lawn and adjacent vegetable garden! He promptly shooed the horses onto the highway, mounted one of his vehicles and chased the horses at high speed almost a mile in the direction of where they were supposed to be pastured. He returned to bed, but by daylight, all of the horses were back.

My family and I were not exempted from the equestrienne night-time visits. My farm was located a half mile from my Brother's house. Except when away from home, we left our garage door open day and night during the summer months. One of our kitchen doors opened into our garage. Early one morning, my Wife was startled out of her wits upon opening the door which bumped into the head of a jackass! In her excitement, she dropped and spilled whatever she was carrying. The jackass was not alone. Also standing there before large piles of manure was a horse! And what was more, there were more horses grazing upon our lawn!

I wasted no time paying the horse vendor an early morning visit. He tried to greet me with some neighborly niceties, but I came abruptly to the point of my visit. I related the incident of my Wife's encounter with the jackass. I stood almost nose to nose with that old coot, waved a finger under his and told him,

"Old man, I'm only going to make this short speech once. If I ever see those flee bag animals on my property again, I will lead them over the mountain in my forest, I will tie them to trees, and let them starve to death! Do I make myself clear?"

My Brother and I were never again bothered by the horses.

My encounter with the old man was not over, never-the-less. My farm was almost equally divided by the highway, The flat land lay atop a broad mountain ridge and sloped off to become steep forested hollows on both sides. One night at eleven o'clock as my family and I were preparing to go to bed, two speeding 'pick-up' trucks came to a skidding stop directly in front of our house. I rushed to a front window in time to see the horse trader and three other men open the doors to dog crates and release a half dozen coon-hounds. The men turned on their electric lanterns and followed the pack of gleefully bellowing hounds across the field in front of our house.

I loaded a shot gun, turned on the front porch light, fired a couple of shots into the air, and shouted, "What is going on down there?"

All of the men came to an abrupt halt. Horse Vendor acted as spokesman for all as he responded, "Oh, we're just going to do a little coon hunting."

"Well," I responded, "You're not going to do any coon hunting on my land tonight nor any other night. Now, you round up that bunch of mangy mutts and your grungy friends and leave before I do some serious shooting,"

Getting back to the widow who was wanting to buy a cow. Apparently Farmer Friendly rounded up one of his range cows who had never had a love affair in her life and hauled her in his truck to the widow's home.

The story as she related it to a friend went this way:

"I hear that you are wanting to buy a cow," Cow Vendor said.
"Yes, that is true," replied the Widow. "Is that cow pregnant?"

Cow Vendor's response was, "Partly."

James E. Martin

SPLITTING HAIR 101

Sometimes we Appalachian folk are credited with having some peculiar ideas. Most of them are quite harmless and amusing at times. Having been reared within the environment where many of those peculiarities abound, I, myself, have been socially mutated by them. As you, the reader, may agree, it is much easier to recognize someone else's pecularities than it is to admit your own. I am certain that in this story which I am about to relate, I am being guilty of exactly that. But, what the Heck. I'm going to write it any way.

The Family about whom I am writing possessed most of the sterling qualities of character and good citizenship upon which we evaluate people. They were honest, truthful, trustworthy, self reliant, generous, helpful, and law-abiding. Besides, the four brothers in that family were my earliest and most abiding friends until death claimed them. They were also some of my earliest school-mates, two of which followed me into high school.

None of us ever took each other very seriously. We knew that we were peculiar. It was mighty hard to act very sophisticated when we lived on hand-labor farms during the 'Great Depression', never seeing a dollar bill, wearing patches upon patches upon patches, and going barefooted during summertime until we were sixteen years old. To prevent us from looking like Australian bushmen, our fathers gave us home made haircuts once every six weeks or so. Fathers were also the family dentists and shoe repairer when we were lucky enough to have shoes.

We who went to high school from our neighborhood had to complete our farm chores before daylight in order to walk the six mile distance to the high school. That didn't leave much time for preening and grooming. On the morning of the second day of the fall semester just after the three of us entered the school's front door, one of the brothers removed a celluloid comb appearing to be almost as large as a garden rake without handle from beneath his shirt. Handing it to his brother, he said, "Here George, split my hair."

THE COAL TOWN TOILET

One of my Uncles worked inside a coal mine located in West Virginia during the early 1930s. There was a time which lasted one or two weeks during which his Supervisor did not need him at his normal work site. The mine Officials were in the process of enlarging the outside work and storage area. Timber-men had cut all of the trees on the level ground where the work area was to be expanded and had removed all of the debris except many large stumps. Although my Uncle's inside the mine duties did not involve the use of explosives and he did not have the slightest knowledge of explosives, his Supervisor told him to draw the dynamite, caps, and fuse cable necessary to blow the stumps out of the ground.

Hoping to learn his new duties quickly, with no major mistakes, and to stay alive in the process, he selected a large maple stump located at the farthest point from the mine and its equipment. He reasoned that, if he succeeded in removing that large stump, he could easily remove any of the smaller ones; besides he thought he could use the experience to better estimate how much dynamite to use under varying circumstances. The stump was near the edge of a hill above some of the gardens and residences of the coal town. In addition to the gardens, behind each house stood a small coal house and an outside toilet built of wood and installed above a pit.

My Uncle had no idea of how much dynamite would be necessary to remove the stump. He merely wished to experiment until he could estimate the power of future shots by increasing the load gradually. Gradually is a term not easily quantified. The stump was massive, so he estimated that six sticks of dynamite should be sufficient. He set the charge and sheltered himself at a safe distance behind a concrete building.

Unknown to him at that very moment, an elderly lady who lived in a house bordering the highway approximately four hundred feet down a hillside below where the stump was located had gone to the family toilet for a morning visit. My Uncle learned later that the lady and her husband were emigrants from Italy. When the explosion occurred, much to my Uncle's dismay, the dynamite extracted that stump like a huge tooth. It soared beautifully high into the air and tumbled lazily to the earth, but alas, it landed on the down slope of the hill. He quickly dashed to the site just in time to see the bounding stump sweep the toilet from its foundation exposing the alarmed lady still sitting upon the toilet seat! Miraculously the lady was uninjured, but the event certainly scared the bejabers out of her. He said that she shouted "Mammamea!", as she gathered her garments about her knees, and ran through her back doorway like all of the demons on earth were after her. Fortunately, the stump missed their house, careened across the highway, and landed in the middle of a wide creek far from its original location.

The story does not end on that day, however. Coal Company carpenters were sent to remove the shattered remains of the out-house, remove the old floor from above the pit, and make plans to install a new one the following day. The kindly old couple owned a gentle Jersey cow which they pastured upon their garden plot instead of growing a garden. The old folk dearly loved that cow like parents would worship a child. During the night, the cow accidentally fell into the toilet pit. When my Uncle came to work the following morning, the cow was still positioned with her hind legs down inside the pit and with her front ones resting upon the surface. The old couple were in morning and tearfully trying to comfort her. Several neighbors arrived carrying ropes. Under the circumstances, plus hygienic considerations being of some concern, it required at least an hour of difficult work for several men to extract the poor animal from her plight. My Uncle said that during mid-afternoon the old couple were still bathing the cow with soapy water and drying her with bath towels while maintaining a grieving dialogue of "Our poor dear Baby!"

UNCOMMON FRACTION

During the mid-1930s when I was in the fourth grade, I spent a considerable amount of school time learning the about the wonderful world of fractions. I did not think that they were especially difficult and I really appreciated their value. Just like most of the other things our one-room school teacher taught me, I was urged to remember that I would be using fractions throughout my every-day adult life some day. That admonition has proven true, of course, but, if true, I reasoned that great 'truth' should have already been ingrained into the practice of those who had already become adults long before myself.

A case in point: The congregation of the little church which my family attended was comprised mostly by farm families such as my own. It was early spring and corn planting time was upon the land. Clustered outside the entrance one Sunday Morning prior to 'starting time' were several farmers engaged in conversation. Children, such as I, were supposed to be seen and not heard, but we were expected to listen and try to learn some gumption. Thus I was listening to two of my neighbors talk about farming.

"Say, Toby," one man asked another, "Is yer corn coming up pretty good?"

"No," answered the other man. "Not good atall. Only about three thirds of it came up."

WEDDED BLISS

There was a time when my Family and I lived at Clarksville, Tennessee. We rented a small house and became close friends with our Landlord and his family. The youngest son married his high school sweetheart when they graduated at age eighteen. They were a cute couple who still seemed like babies to we twenty nine year olds. Both of the newly-weds were so very innocent and unworldly having hardly traveled outside their small home town, but they had good parents upon whose wisdom and guidance they could rely. Sadly, misfortune struck twenty five years later when the young wife suddenly died.

We spent many light-hearted days with that family, days which we recall when our own children were young. Those good times seem as though they happened only yesterday. One such memory always causes my Wife and I to chuckle.

One afternoon approximately two weeks after the young couple's marriage, the Mother and a Sister of the Groom took the Bride grocery shopping with them. They also invited my Wife to go with them. The family's favorite shopping location was an old fashioned general store only a few blocks from their home. In addition to an adequate supply of groceries, the interior of the store contained the wide shelves so typical of old stores ranging along the full length of three walls and reaching from the floor to the ceiling. A ladder attached at the top to a roller track enabled a person to reach the high shelves to remove merchandise. The building was quite large and was also equipped with all of the modern coolers and freezers, etc.

It was obvious to the older women that the young bride had very little experience grocery shopping. They were amused by some of her comments, questions, and purchases. Having satisfied their needs, the older women were waiting their turns at the checkout counter when the bride gave everyone present a hilarious moment when she plopped an old-fashioned white enamel coated chamber pot complete with lid upon a counter top and proclaimed for all to hear, "Look what I found. A bean pot! My husband just loves beans!"

Her flabbergasted sister-in-law gasped, "Rose Mary, that is not a bean pot. That is a chamber mug!"

James E. Martin

THE FEED STORE

My Wife and I were living in Charleston, West Virginia. I had retired from the United States Army and had returned to Morris Harvey College to complete a Bachelor Degree in Geography which I had began in 1946 after being discharged from the Army the first time. My education was interrupted by the outbreak of the Korean War, when I was recalled to duty. I stayed until retirement in June 1968.

We really like Charleston, but the chemical odors in the air were a great irritant to my throat and sinuses, so we were contemplating returning to the mountains of our origin in Greenbrier County. I had no particular plans, so the return was made easy when I received a call from my Brother one night informing me that the manager of his feed store in Rainelle had given him a two week notice that he was resigning. My Brother was in panic, because he, himself, could not abandon other enterprises in which engaged to take over management of the store. So, why not? I accepted his offer.

There was something nostalgic about that dusty old feed store. I had spent my youth on a farm seven miles south-east of Rainelle at a time before paved roads, supermarkets, and rural electricity. Those were the days of one-room schools, grist mills, and country stores/Post Offices located at the intersections of most main roads. The times of cashless barter for store-bought needs. Days of horses, wagons, and early open-top jalopies. Days when nail kegs, rocking chairs, and platform scales shared the old store porches with the Neighbors whittling, chewing tobacco, and telling lies. The Age when customers filled their 'Old Tin lizzies' at the upright ten-gallon hand pumped gas tanks and was taken at their word when they entered the store and told the Merchant how much gas they had gotten. Those were the times when children found excitement spending Saturday afternoons playing marbles in the fine road-side dust in front of the old country stores. There were horseshoe games pitched until mid-night by the light of lanterns hung upon fence posts adjacent to the pegs. I especially enjoyed sitting atop a zig zag rail fence watching the men from visiting communities playing the 'locals' a baseball game in the hayfield behind my Uncle Orph's store at Crag.

Upon arriving at my new job, I was pleased to learn that many of the older neighbors whom I knew and loved still survived the many years since I had known them as a child. It was also rewarding to me to be reunited with many of the men my age who never planned to leave their homesteads, but as myself, were drafted into military service. All, as I, came back home war-weary, some disabled, but most were content to return to the roots of their origin. I discovered that many of the old home sites were still in use, although somewhat modernized. Of course, modern cars and trucks had replaced the horses and wagons of yesterday, only a few dirt roads remained, but the family tradition of coming to town on Saturday prevailed. Unlike the country stores and one-room school houses of nevermore, that little feed store was like an Icon, a vestige of the contented past. I felt so privileged to see the scene pass before my eyes once more with many of the same Actors still upon the stage.

True to the heritage of those earlier days, the humorous aspects of operating a country store still survived during the days of the 1970s. Some of those incidents shall remain vivid to me as long as I live. I shall take pleasure from relating some of them to you now.

The store building was first used as a small cinema beginning during the 1920s and lasting to the late 1930s. A larger more modern theater caused it to close prior to World War II. A local resident rented the building from its Owner, partitioned off a sales room and created a warehouse area for feed, fertilizer, cement, and large hardware items such as rolls of fencing wire. Many items of mixed merchandise including paint, chain saws, seeds, veterinary medicines, hand tools, and agricultural chemicals occupied the sales room. The original merchant died, so his Wife offered the feed business for sale.

My Brother, himself having returned home from military service, purchased the feed store as an adjunct to his cattle and chicken business. By the time my Brother purchased it, the feed store had become a tradition. Traditions are created to endure, so this one was no exception. When my Brother also died several years later, his Family sold the business. The new owner continued the tradition until competition from large corporate outlets forced his to close during 1996.

There is something very earthy and inviting about a feed store. Although it was not a fancy place, nothing else can compare with the delicious aroma of many kinds of feed blending with the smells of salt, fertilizer, leather goods, and veterinary supplies. Add to that the constant odors emitted from the coffee pot and the wafting of pipe and cigar smoke about the room. Their allure engenders memories of old country stores, grist mills, barbershops, livery stables, and blacksmith shops.

Several people were usually present throughout the business day. It made no difference if a person came to make a purchase or just to rest a bit. A spirited but good humored discussion was in progress about current events, religion, or politics much of the time. Great quantities chewing tobacco was consumed and disposed of. Much time was spent trading knives and espousing tall tales which were always claimed to be true.

The majority of feed store customers were men, because they were most closely involved with the caring and feeding of animas. The lifting of fifty and one hundred pound bags of feed also required considerable strength. We sold great volumes of pet food, however, much of which was purchased by women and children. The little people especially enjoyed visiting the feed store during early springtime when baby rabbits, ducklings, and chicks were for sale.

During spring planting season, I had to hire extra helpers to serve the constant lines of people buying live plants and garden seeds. At those times, most people were in too much of a hurry to stand about talking. On Saturday afternoons, however, the traditional 'Old Residences' of winter would reappear to sit and visit.

There was one Customer who bought many thousands of dollars worth of merchandise each year. He owned a huge farm and had raised a large family. He spent many Saturday afternoons at the store greatly enjoying the lively conversations. In addition to farming, he had spent a career working inside coal mines with low ceilings. His back hurt so that he used a cane and he walked bent at his waist in such a manner that his back was horizontal with the ground. Upon entering the store and using the top of a sales counter for support, he could force himself up to more than six feet in height.

By nature, a feed store is usually a dusty place. I provided enough light to adequately conduct business and to see my Customers, but it was far from being illuminated like the façade of a Las Vegas casino. I kept the sales room as neat and clean as possible under the circumstances by giving the floor a daily sweeping. The main sales counter had a glass front behind which I displayed an assortment of knives, ammunition, watches, etc. Each Saturday morning, I made that glass front spotless using window cleaner. I had cleaned it thoroughly one Saturday before that valued Customer came in. A group of men were engaged in a discussion of religious theory when he arrived. He was standing as usual beside the glass fronted counter with his right arm resting on its top as he listened intently to the discussion. Ignoring the sawdust filled metal box resting upon the floor at his feet for collecting tobacco juice, he curled his lips into a small tight circle and spat a generous squirt of tobacco juice kersplat diagonally across the face of my clean glass! Simultaneously, he jumped right into the discussion with a thunderous proclamation, "Ornless ye air ah 'blood warshed Christian' ye'll never see th pearly gates of Heaven!"

There were many colorful Citizens who patronized the feed store. I treated each of them with equal respect, however, I found some of them far more interesting than others. I was especially intrigued by one man. My Brother had informed me that he was peculiar, but honest. He was also one of the store's most loyal customers. I was asked to look beyond his appearance, treat him with respect, and to honor his requests for special treatment.

The man lived within a compound which he erected upon his hillside property just outside the Town limits. His neighbors did not live in harmony with him, partly because of his eccentricities, but mostly because he provided sanctuary to any and all stray dogs looking for a home. At times, it was reported that more than a dozen dogs lived there. Neighbors complained that the dogs were kept under no constrains, so they wandered freely all over town making a nuisance of themselves. Neighbors also complained that it was impossible to sleep because of the barking dogs. Is it any surprise that the man was the store's highest volume dog food customer?

Well, the story was told that he was also the whiskey store's highest volume customer. It was that bit of information that prompted Brother to alert me to 'The Arrangement.' The arrangement had been established long before I began working at the store. That strange person lived on a retirement pension and, at times, overspent his resources before the end of the month payday arrived. The 'arrangement' was that should he request a small loan, which never exceeded ten dollars, I was to grant his request and record the amount on his 'tab.' Those requests never occurred more than twice per month. Brother told me not to fret and, should he request dog food on credit, also grant that request.

True to Brother's prediction, the customer came in and paid his account in full the first working day of each month. He would then have me charge him for ten twenty five pound bags of dog food, place them outside the front door upon the sidewalk, and he would have a friend with a truck pick them up before closing time.

I discovered early in my new career that product knowledge was extremely important in the feed business, since farm customers rely upon the merchant to be a sort of 'hayseed guru.' To fill that expectation, I used every opportunity to study and remember information on labels and in trade bulletins. Some of that information was rather technical, especially that pertaining to veterinary medicines, herbicides, and pest control chemicals. Most customer questions were non-technical. Some were amusing, such as the one which came by phone one morning.

"Good morning, how may I help you?" I asked.

Without the formality of a greeting, the caller came directly to the point, "Hey! Ah don't reckon ye have ary bit of that there grass that grows up next to th house do ya?"

I didn't have a clue of what he was talking about, but, armed with the knowledge that we stocked every type of grass suitable for planting in that Region, I assured him, "Yes, we have."

He said, "Thankie." and hung up.

Our customers were allowed to go freely to any part of the store unescorted so that they could privately examine our merchandise at will. That is the way feed stores are. One day when I was working alone, I had just taken a female customer two bags of feed and loaded it into her car. I was returning a two-wheeled dock truck to the warehouse when I observed a teen-aged girl holding one of the swinging warehouse doors halfway open. She had a quart-sized milkshake cup in one hand and had a soda straw stuck inside her mouth.

I parked the dock truck and asked, "May I help you?"

"Ya kin help him," she mumbled without removing the soda straw from her mouth and nodded her head toward the inside of the warehouse.

I had received a tractor trailer load of bagged feed the previous day, so it was stacked to the ceiling with four foot wide walkway between stacks. I pulled the remaining swinging door open so I could see to whom she referred, but I saw no one. I looked back at the girl and she said, "Him."

"Him whom?" I questioned as I took a couple of steps further into the warehouse. To my surprise, standing there between the stacks with one hand resting upon a bag of sweet horse feed stood a midget!

Before I could recover my composure, the man spoke with a broad slow drawl, "He-e-e-y, is this here stuff good for stuff?"

"What do you mean?" I asked trying not to show my surprise.

"Wa-a-a-l," he retorted, his attitude becoming a bit testy. "It's horse nure, ain't it!"

I had difficulty suppressing my amusement and blurted out, "Why do you think that?"

Thumping the bag forcefully with four fingers of one hand to show his disgust with my total lack of logic, he stormed, "Eny danged fool ken plain see that the poke has a pitcher of a horse on it!"

One spring morning I was busy selling bulk orders of garden seeds. The line of customers waiting at the scales reached all the way through the sidewalk. Suddenly, a middle-aged woman accompanied by a younger one, stridently shoved her way past those standing in the doorway and came to the head of the line at the scales where I was totaling a sale.

Rudely interrupting me, she asked, "Can you tell me the difference between top soil and cow manure?"

Amid a flurry of snickers from the crowd, I concluded that a stupid question deserved an equally stupid answer. Trying to strike my best back-country deep-thinker pose, I reached my right arm across my head, began scratching my scalp just above my left ear, screwed my face up in mock sincerity as though I was hoping for a flash of divine wisdom, and drawled, "Waal, th way ah understand it, cow manure comes outta a cow and top soil is just a natural part of the Earth."

As though satisfied with some preordained concept, she said, "That's exactly what I wanted to know." That having been said, she turned on a heel and stomped out of the room past the gleeful on-lookers followed closely once more by the younger woman.

A retarded man approximately twenty five years of age lived in an adjoining village. He was incapable of earning a living and was totally dependent upon his sister for his support. She had to earn a living, so she reasoned that he could survive upon the streets each day until she came home from work. She made an arrangement with the owner of a hamburger shop to feed him daily and she would pay his debt weekly. The extremely filthy smelly fellow paced the streets back ward and forward from the east end of Rainelle to a Dairy Queen located a block past the feed store throughout the entire business days Monday through Friday each week. No business place would allow him to enter, because to do so, he would become a pest. The hamburger man handed his food to him from the back door of his shop. Obviously endowed with an insatiable appetite, the young man repeatedly raided trash cans along his entire 'route' scrounging for scraps of food and partially filled milkshake cups and bottles. He always needed a shave. His rusty colored beard and the front of his clothing were smeared by a mixture of food and beverages. His troubled mind must have been obsessed by visions of a pending disastrous 'flash flood'. Especially during summer months as he passed the feed store's open door, he would shout "frash frud."

From my office window, I had a clear view of the sidewalk and street. I was taking advantage of a lull in business one morning by sitting at my desk and catching up on a backlog of paper work when I saw a young woman parking her car wearing Ohio license plates at the first meter adjacent to our loading zone. Just as she deposited a coin in the meter and was turning to leave, she collided chest to chest with that grungy man! It happened in a mili-second as her face registered both surprise and disgust. When he flung both hands up palms forward inches from her face, breathed his terrible breath on her, and shouted "Woo woo!", she screamed and fled in terror. I do not know if that incident or possibly many more hastened the man's departure from the town's streets, but shortly following it, I didn't see him again.

Having been gone from Greenbrier County for most of twenty five years, I knew that many of the elderly people whom I had known as a child were no longer alive. You can imagine my mixture of joy and surprise when an 'old-timer' whom I had assumed to be dead, walked into the store one day! We had a grand reunion. He informed me that he was past ninety-five years old. That night, I visited my Parents. During dinner, I made the exciting announcement about meeting our old family friend at the feed store that day.

"He told me that he was over ninety-five years old!" I exclaimed.

As quick as lightning, my Mother shot back, "Yes, and that old whiskey is going to kill him!"

There was another 'old residenter' who came into the store on an infrequent basis. He lived past his one hundred and third birthday before dying during 1999. He and his family were distant neighbors of my family when I was a child. One of his daughters told me an interesting story about her Father and one of his friends. Her Father had discontinued driving, but relied upon family and friends to take him where he wished to go. It was at the time when Interstate 64 was incomplete from Alta to Beckley, West Virginia. The highway was being completed only a few miles at a time before being opened to traffic. The local news media announced the opening of a seven mile segment from Lewisburg to Alta.

This lady's Father and a neighbor bought and sold cattle. They were also the closest of friends. On most Saturdays, they attended the auction at the Caldwell Livestock Market near Lewisburg. Apparently neither of the men had heard about the opening of the road. Her Father said that he noticed it as they approached the West-bound exit ramp. He said, "Look there, they've opened the new road. Lets take it."

Being unfamiliar with Interstate Highways, they entered the Westbound lane going the wrong way. After traveling only a few hundred yards, her father said to his friend, "Look, they have made another road just like this one."

Not much farther along, they met a highway patrolman. He stopped them and announced that they were going the wrong way, turned them around, and sent them down the proper lane. That was bad enough, but he told her that they made the same mistake the following Saturday. That time, they went all of the way, but did not encounter any policemen.

The late 1970s was a time when the National Football League's Baltimore Colts were my favorite team. I had given my Wife and children stern warning that they could be eliminated from my last will if they interrupted my concentration while I watched a Sunday afternoon Colts game. Well, one Sunday afternoon the unthinkable happened! My Wife risked the direst of fate by announcing to me that some female feed store customer wished to speak to me on the telephone. The game had less than a minute to go. The game was tied ten to ten. The Colts had their opponent on the latter's one yard line. It was fourth down and the clock was running. I WAS ENRAGED!

I struggled for some degree of composure and civility when I answered the call.

Without the courtesy of identifying herself, a voice shrill with frustration demanded, "Can you tell me the degree of my slope?"

With that, I came unglued. "Are you crazy, woman?" I roared. "Are you some kind of a nut? You interrupt my football game on a Sunday to ask me some crack-pot question like that! What on Earth are you talking about?"

"No, I just want someone to tell me the degree of my slope," she insisted.

I was trying to imagine some logical reason that a sane person would have to justify such a stupid question. That is when it occurred to me that the woman must be trying to answer the questions on a soil-test application.

"Are you submitting a soil-test to the University?" I asked.

"Yes, I am," she replied. "They ask what is the degree of my slope. What does that mean?"

I explained how to answer the question and she was satisfied, but by the time the conversation was over, so was the game. The television station had completed its post-game comments, so I had to await the sports segment of the late evening news broadcast to learn the outcome of the game.

_____ · _____

Twenty seven years have passed since I began work at the feed store, but many of my fond memories remain. Had I not accepted my Brother's invitation to manage the store, I would not have been afforded the opportunity to step back into the environment of my childhood and to share Life's stage with many of the same players who were a part of the original Cast. Perhaps I should feel sad as I realize that those pleasant days are forever absorbed by a quarter century of the past, but I don't. I look at life as a continual opportunity to expand my life experience, each minute revealing that which is exciting and new.

I feel thankful for the Fate which recast me into that happy scene. It was a mirror image of the Era so beautifully described by poets such as Longfellow, Whittier, and Riley; and by artists such as Norman Rockwell. If I have regrets, they are that the majority of Americans much younger than I will never have opportunity to experience the horse and buggy days, that wonderful Age in our Nation's History.

Now what?

SOME DAYS ARE LIKE THAT

The Christmas Season of 1944 was ending and I was due to report back to my Army Unit at Fort Bragg, North Carolina. I had recently returned from overseas the first time and was on my first furlough since being drafted during 1942. I had returned home carrying a full load of home-sickness, so being home for Christmas was especially rewarding for me.

I had grown to adulthood on a mountain farm located in Western Greenbrier County, West Virginia where the winters during the decade of the 1920s through the 1940s were typified by the harshest weather which I can remember. It came as no surprise to me when three days before I was to return to Fort Bragg, a miserable storm consisting of both deep snow and ice coating most of the Eastern United States. Vehicular travel was almost impossible. I became worried that I would be able to return to my Army Unit on time to avoid being AWOL, so I asked my Father to take me to Rainelle a day early where I could catch the first south-bound bus at daybreak.

As was customary in our farm community, we and our neighbors spent a day using scoop shovels clearing the two-mile unpaved road to Crag where other citizens cleared similar segments of the seven mile route to Rainelle. Should a medical emergency occur, country folk could reach help. The only trouble remaining was that a foggy drizzle covered the land with ice.

My father owned a log truck upon which he and I installed dual chains. The commuter bus was due in Rainelle at seven o'clock AM, so we left home at 4:30 AM hoping that we could travel the hilly roadway to Rainelle in time for me to board the bus. It was no great problem to climb the steep grades with the heavy truck equipped with chains, but descending the steep grades was scary. To avoid crashing, my Father positioned the truck in the up-side ditches to avoid sliding off the road into deep ravines. Thus the chains provided enough traction to allow the truck to safely follow the side-ditches to the bottom of the hills.

We arrived at the bus station with some time to spare. I began to see the wisdom of leaving a day early when the bus arrived. The driver, who had also been driving across mountains, stated that he had been advised that making on-time connections with main-line carriers was going to be difficult. Most were running very late.

I took comfort when I noted that the commuter bus was also equipped with chains and that the Highway Department had spread gravel upon the major road. Major roads during that era did not mean that they were 'wide' roads. They were just two lanes and were not very wide at all. What was most disturbing to me was that to reach Beckley (approximately forty miles distance) via Meadow Bridge, Danese, Layland, and Prince necessitated climbing two long steep mountain grades and descending one. I was so glad that the commuter bus was equipped with dry sand dispensing devices in front of each rear wheel as well as having the chains installed. Although we arrived at Beckley without mishap, it required all the skill that that driver could muster just to keep the bus upon the pavement.

The Greyhound Bus from Charleston, West Virginia to Winston-Salem, North Carolina was at least an hour behind schedule. The driver appeared to be exhausted from the ordeal of climbing into the high country surrounding Beckley. Ahead lay lofty Flat Top Mountain before reaching Princeton and enormous Big Walker Mountain beyond Bluefield, before reaching Hillsville, Virginia not counting dozens of smaller hills along the way.

Everyone on board had hopped that the ice would disappear as we traveled farther South, but that was not to be. During the late afternoon, having traveled with great difficulty, but without accident, we were in sight of the small town of Hillsville, Virginia. As we were beginning to climb the last small hill outside of town, I could see people standing in front of a small restaurant at its summit. A rather deep cut had been made in the hill to moderate the road grade when building it. The resulting bank was approximately fifteen feet high. A shallow concave ditch with a shale bottom ran the entire length of the bank. The bus had reached mid-point of the hill, but as its wheels were spinning forward, the bus was slowly sliding backward. It slid off the pavement and found the ditch as it neared the bottom of the hill without apparent danger. The bus driver was frantically wrestling with the wheel.

A small but ancient lady had boarded the bus in Bluefield. The bus was not crowded, but she chose to sit alone on a seat near the rear of the bus, having hardly spoken a word to anyone. Some of those standing at the top of the hill may have been there to meet her, Hillsville possibly being her destination. Whatever her motivation after such a harried trip, as the bus began its backward slide down the side-ditch, she gathered her brocade cloth satchel and walked as silently as a kitten to where the driver was struggling with the steering wheel.

The little lady gently tapped the driver upon a shoulder and said, "Sonny, if you will please stop the bus, I'd like to get off."

Struggling for composure, the frustrated bus driver responded with a bellowing voice, "Lady, If I can stop this bus, we'll all get off!"

PASTLOGUE: The bus stopped of its own accord at the bottom of the hill without damage and all passengers debarked safely. Another man and I assisted the little lady as we followed the gravel ditch to the top of the hill. The bus driver called for a wrecker. The lady met her kin and we all at a meal at the restaurant. And, yes. The ice was gone by the time we reached the town of Mount Airy, North Carolina at the foot of Fancy Gap Mountain. And I reached Fort Bragg on time.

GOURMET SOUP

I spent a total of one hundred twenty days aboard US Navy transport vessels to reach several changes of US Army duty stations during World War II. I am certain that my presence on board did not make any lasting impact upon the Navy, but the experiences I had left many durable memories for me. Sea sickness, crowded decks, hot stinking quarters deep inside the hull, culvert-like toilets thirty seats long perpetually half filled with water which would rise up to kiss my butt as the ship lurched from side to side, the worst chow on earth, consisting of clumpy powdered eggs which were the consistency of dehydrated cow pies, but colored blue. Reconstituted powdered milk that looked, smelled, and perhaps tasted like calamine lotion. Oatmeal that could stand in a corner or, if rolled flat, could pave a highway. Corned beef hash that a hyena wouldn't eat. And, oh yes, Baked beans and cornbread for Tuesday morning breakfasts! Add to that wonderful environment U-boat attacks at night, bomber attacks during daytime, and typhoons which last for days, it was a cinch one would see no talent scouts recruiting for the 'Love Boat' employees.

Now, to Mariners, the line which I am preparing to tell you may be as old as Davy Jones, but I am going to tell it any way, because it added the only modicum of humor I can recall throughout my brief sea life. One day, some joker attempting to bring some levity to an otherwise mirthless world announced over the public address system, "Now hear this. Master At Arms, lay the Duty Chicken down to the galley. The cook wants to trot it through the soup."

WHERE'S THE BEEF?

A Country Church located several miles from where I live held a banquet inside the church's fellowship hall. It was one of those 'covered dish' affairs where by each family could bring whatever kind of food they wished. A rather wealthy and successful cattle farmer was a member of that church. He announced that he would furnish beef from his farm for all of the large number of people planning to attend the dinner. That impressed the planners as a generous offer, which they gratefully accepted.

The fellowship hall was filled to capacity on the night of the banquet, which was declared to be a great success. The Chairperson of the Planning Committee was graciously thanking all whom had participated for their generous cooperation, singling out many persons who had been especially helpful. The cattle farmer was thanked profusely for what was considered the most generous contribution of all. He was, therefore, asked to stand to be honored and was requested to speak a few words. He rose to his feet, acknowledged the applause of those present and made the following brief comment:

"Aw shucks, twaren't nothing cose t'was a pity to just let er lay there and the buzzards eat er."

OLD LAM

On or about year 1926, my Grandfather, Perry Lonzo Martin owned and operated a sawmill at the site which later became the coal town of Anjean, West Virginia. Before the sawmill could be installed, it was necessary for the timber men to clear a trail through dense forest along the banks of Little Clear Creek for a distance of approximately six miles from the small settlement of Rupert to the base of a mountain named Cold Knob. Horses were used to pull the sawmill's steam engine and wagon loads of other mill components along the dirt trail to the mill site.

Two wealthy brothers, John and Tom Raines, had purchased thousands of acres of coal and timber land in Greenbrier, Nicholas, and Fayette Counties where they later established dozens of deep mines, built railroads, created the largest hard-wood lumber mill in America, and built the Greenbrier County town of Rainelle, bearing their family name.

The initial mine was opened at the Western foot of Cold Knob. Grandfather was contracted to clear the Anjean Town site, mill the timber into lumber for the town's houses, the structural beams for the coal tipple, and the crossties for the railroad.

Imagine yourself being the first human to wander into that vast forest surrounded by ferns whose tops were as high as an adult's head and by trees more than eighty feet tall standing close together like the bristles of a brush. Many of the trees were over seven feet in diameter. The forest and the mountains upon which it grew had stood there undisturbed for millions of years. Only the Indians and perhaps an occasional pioneer may have ever passed that spot. If you were standing there alone, the solitude would be overwhelming, the silence broken only by the wind, the birds, and water splashing over rocks in the streams. It is probable that there was not another human nor a residence straight ahead fifty miles North at the time the men cleared that first trail. The virgin forests are gone now, but there are news stories each year about hunters and hikers becoming lost in that vast wilderness area.

It was into that setting that Grandfather 'Lon' installed his sawmill. Soon the deep silence was broken by the sounds of chopping axes, the pinging of steel hammers striking wedges, the merry tinkle of rings, buckles, and chains on the harnesses of horses as they moved along the logging roads. One could have heard the voices of men as they talked, gave commands to the horses, or shouted the warning, 'TIMBER!", when giant trees were ready to crash to the ground. New sounds were added with the arrival of each day. Soon, the sawmill was completely assembled and operating. The huff, puff, and pant of the stationary engine could now be heard as it chugged, sweated, and hissed while belching fluffy white clouds of steam, showers of crackling sparks, and belching billowing black smoke from its tall stack. The rapidly spinning large red-spoked drive wheel made a whirring sound as it transmitted power to the mill through the violently bouncing drive belt. The sound of high speed saw teeth ripping into a log emitted high-pitched z-z-z-z a-wa-a-a-ah screeches which would cause unprotected ears to ring. By comparison, the clapping of heavy wide boards being dropped upon stacks sounded like a distant echo. The shrill whistle of the steam engine, combined with all of the other noises, created the illusion of some weird woodland orchestra playing a concert.

In a few weeks, the sound of carpenters' hammers blended with all of the others as construction of the new town began. The first building was a large bunk house with kitchen and dining room where the timber men could eat and sleep. Grandfather Lon hired several women to cook, clean house, make beds, and wash laundry. He appointed his eldest Son to be bookkeeper and paymaster. The sawmill was producing large amounts of lumber. The carpenters built many dwellings, a store, school, church, barbershop, shoe repair shop, blacksmith shop, and stables. A large coal tipple was also constructed astride the railhead where the coal cars could be loaded.

Dozens of men were digging the tunnel into the side of the mountain to reach the coal. Within a few months, several hundred people were living at Anjean. There was an ever-increasing demand for lumber, so it was necessary for Grandfather to hire many more laborers. That brings me to the heart of this story.

During the pre- Great Depression days, many immigrants were entering the United States to fill the needs of our industrial expansion. Due greatly to the vast disruption of family life, educational opportunity, and availability of employment, many immigrants sought to just get a foothold in a new land in any manner they could.

Many were willing to fill positions of common labor just to accomplish that. 'Old Lam' was such a man. He was uneducated, but he was not dumb. The needs for laborers was so great that employers such as Grandfather and the Raines brothers did not care what a man's name was or where he came from. They only wanted to know if a man was willing and able to work. In exchange for that, they would pay him a wage and provide him food and lodging.

Some men who knew Old Lam best said that he came from Poland. Of course, Lam was not his real name. That was the name his fellow workers gave him, because they could not pronounce his real name. When you think about it, the name Lam does not make any real sense. You understand, most timber men of that era also were ignorant and uneducated as a rule. They often used terms which they had dreamed up and only they could comprehend to describe something. For example: If someone hit or struck something, they would say, "He lamed it."

Old Lam's job winter and summer was to drive a team of huge horses dragging logs from the forest to the mill. Good quality waterproof winter foot wear had not been developed at that time, so just as did all of the men who worked long days out of doors wearing leaky leather shoes while wading the mud and snow of West Virginia's extremely cold winters, Lam had to do whatever he could to prevent his feet from freezing.

His co-workers observed that the first thing that Lam would do upon entering the forest each morning was halt his team, walk to the nearest stump, and kick it several times with each foot to increase circulation of his blood. That became such a habit that Lam would even do it during the warm days of summer. The stump kicking amused the other men who would pause to watch the old man 'lam' the stump. That is how he got his name.

There was, however, something very special and beautiful about Lam's daily ritual. He brought from his native Poland what can best be described as a poem, which he always recited as the kicked a stump. Over several years of life in America, he learned to speak these words in English:

> Old blue Monday
> Cruel Tuesday
> Everlasting Wednesday
> Thursday never will come
> Friday, is this you?
> Sweet Saturday
> Sunday last forever!

When the sawmill contract was completed, many of the employees drifted away to find other work. Old Lam was among them. My Family does not know what became of that kind old man with the eternally cold feet and poetry in his heart, but where ever it is that old men go, I hope that he has warm dry feet and that his Sundays last forever.

THE OLD HOUSE AT THE CROSSROADS

Moldering, unfinished, vacant, neglected
The weathered old house at the crossroads
Beneath sagging roof, broken beams projected
Casting jagged shadows upon brambly lawn un-mowed
Dreams long abandoned, incomplete
Finished rooms only two of eight
Nineteenth Century newsprint papered their walls
Barn swallows nested in the halls
Glass shards daggered window openings and doors
Rough mill-run boards comprised the floors

Ruins of fence defined the ancient plot
Around the two-story L-shaped edifice which both
    man and time forgot
Untended fields a wilderness of thorns and briars
Overgrowing remnants of abandoned implements
    and cars
Sagging barnyard buildings in disrepair
Half-dead fruit trees scattered here and there
Perched atop a well was a broken hand operated pump
An axe without handle embedded in a decaying stump
One hinge held up the picket gate, entrance to the yard
Rusty chain with a plowshare attached for weight formerly
    used to close it hard

Weed covered enamel chamber pot outside the back yard
fence
Classic two-holed privy reposed a discreet distance hence
Of architectural norm throughout the Country
A two-hole model in the event the User had unexpected

James E. Martin

Company
Pleasure of perusing outdated catalogues used there
Rivaled serenity of finest libraries with their sophisticated
    aire
If those walls could only speak of leisurely time spent
Or of urgent speed approaching world-class record sprint
And balmy days of Summer sweet
Or mid-night dashes through Winter gales of snow and sleet

To that crossroads house my Family came
To clean, repair, to take a stand
The only way we could go was up t'was plain
As 'The Great Depression' gripped the Land
Hard work, soap and water; that is what we used
Hardship and poverty rendered us un-subdued
We were more fortunate than many, we did not whine
Had shelter of sorts and farm food was fine
Shared with those in need what we had to give
Followed the 'Golden Rule' as our way to live

During Winter's wrath slight difference the cold inside
    our house and barn
The open faced fire pit was a poor place to get warm
We warmed one side at a time before the flame
Then rotated to warm the other side the same
From my bed I saw moon and stars through gaping cracks
In sifted snow upon my bedroom floor I made barefoot
tracks
The drinking water bucket and dipping ladle
Froze solid with ice upon the kitchen table
With a corncob soaked with kerosene I'd light the fires
Before visiting the barn to do my chores

Such was our home for many years
We grew healthy, self-reliant, and tough
Over loss of Friends and Family we shed tears
No self pity for being poor; we didn't expect much
Most of what we used was homemade
Our greatest pleasure was time relaxing in the shade
With Family and Friends who came to sit
To spin yarns, to sing, and picnic
We voiced Thanks for survival of what we went through
And strengthened our Resolve with each day anew

The old house is gone, as are the old folks too
Including my Brother and many other Friends I knew
I am so blessed to have experienced the time
From childhood to a long post adult prime
Ah! Those many difficult days I can still recall
In retrospect were not so unpleasant at all
But rather a Time of Heaven on Earth
When a Man's word was his bond and door locks
        were few
A time when we had a clearer view of Life's true worth
And the Old House At The Crossroads was new

James E. Martin

RUSTY

Some people say that there is no greater love than that
between a boy and his dog. There was no shortage of love
between my Dog Rusty and I. This story began during the
summer of 1929 shortly after I was taken in by my foster
family to live on a mountain-top farm seven miles from
Rainelle in Greenbrier County, West Virginia. I was eight
and one half years old at the time I was taken from the State
Orphan's Home at Elkins. Except for a little toy fire truck,
which I had worn out and buried as treasure upon the
grounds at the Orphanage, I had never owned anything,
even the clothing which I wore. I arrived at my new home
barefooted and without as much as a toothbrush or a comb.

My new home was in a dilapidated L-shaped tow-story
unfinished shack of a house with sagging porches and
covered on the outside by unpainted clap-board siding. It
was a typical house of that area without indoor plumbing,
nor had rural electrification yet been introduced. No
furnace, telephone, radio. Meals were cooked on a cast iron
wood-burning stove and the only other room of eight which
was heated in any manner was the living room heated by an
open-faced fire place with a stone chimney. The lawn
surrounding the house was bounded by a wooden fence five
boards high to keep the farm animals out. The house was
located at the intersection of three dirt roads. The sections
of the road near the house were lined buy a mixture of
maple and cherry trees. From that high mountain location,
one could see across valleys and distant peaks, some of

which were twenty miles away. It was into this strange, wild, and beautiful place that I came to live.

At the time that I came to the farm, my new Family owned a pretty long-haired black and white border collie named Lady. She had been trained to herd cattle, which she dearly loved to do. To prevent her from roaming at night, she was tied by a chain attached to the board fence adjacent to her dog-house located just inside the lawn. Shortly after my arrival, Lady gave birth to five puppies. Three of them were black and white like their mother, but the other two were a rusty shade of brown. One brown one was a male with white chest, four white feet, and a white tip on his tail. They grew rapidly and appeared to be as wide as they were long. I liked all of them, but especially the brown male. My new Parents said that I could have him for my own, but homes would have to be found for the others. Well, I knew how that felt. I named the little brown male Rusty and I told my folks that he was the one I wanted.

Rusty's mother was very protective of her little family. Any time a farm animal came near her dog-house, she would chase the intruder away. An animal must have come near Lady's house one night while she was tied by her chain. She must have jumped the fence in order to scare the animal away, but her chain was not long enough for her to reach the ground on the other side. When I entered the back lawn the following morning, I found Lady dead from strangulation.

At his tender age, Rusty was now the dog of the farm. We were inseparable. The only places that Rusty did not go with me were to church, school, and to bed. I would have gladly taken him with me to bed, but my Mother would not allow that. Every day of each year, the first thing I saw in the morning and the last at night was my friend Rusty. We never grew tired of running, playing, and wrestling upon the ground.

Everyone living at the farm had work to do. Although we spent much time playing, neither of us were spared our share of the work. Rusty had to develop into a herd dog. I was given the task of teaching him. Patiently, I taught his to come when called, to stay when told to remain in place, and to circle animals to move them in the right direction. The dog learned to respond to silent hand signals and he learned the meaning of certain whistles. One of Rust's favorite chores was to keep the chickens and turkeys out of the lawn and vegetable garden. He never treated them roughly, but he delighted is seeing them run, flap their wings, and squawk as they scurried to get away from him. He had one mischievous pleasure, however. He delighted in herding all of the chickens from the barnyard and then circling the chicken house until every one of them were inside, following which he would lie in front of the door, keeping them inside. Because of that little trick, my Mother had to scold him. If he kept the chickens penned up, they could not go to the fields to eat. Never-the-less, the Family was amused to see him quietly herding chickens.

The farm is almost a mile in length with all of the crop fields located on the flat top of the mountain and the pasture land on the steep mountain sides. During the cold winter months, the animals would return to the barnyard to be fed morning and night. Their summertime habits were much different, since they found all that they needed to eat by grazing they saw no reason to return to the barn of their own free will. The grazing land also contained many large trees where the animals could relax in shade. We wanted the sheep, cattle, and horses to return home each day so that we could count them and make certain that none were sick or injured. Of special interest were the cows which we milked both morning and evening. Without a herd dog, some family member would have to walk two round trips to the extremities of the farm seven days per week.

Driving the animals was something Rusty loved to do. On a single trip, he would round up every animal on the farm, thus herding one large group back to the barn yard. Early during his training period, he and I would romp down the mountain sides together. As I grew older, I assumed more adult type responsibilities such as tending the garden, weeding the corn field, harvesting crops, husking corn, cutting firewood, and feeding the hogs and poultry.

Rusty soon discovered that he was perfectly happy rounding up the animals by himself. Near four o'clock each afternoon, he sensed that it was time for his evening chore. He would stand several feet in front of me and slowly wag his fluffy tail and make soft woof woof sounds. He seemed to say that it was time to go and was waiting for me to give him the command. I would say, "Rusty, go get the cows!"

He would dash off at an easy gallop at first then settle to a slow single footed trot with his beautiful tail bobbing back and forth. He never got into a hurry. He would circle behind the most distant animal, walk close behind, and bark a couple of times to start the animal walking toward home. He would repeat that action until he had the entire herd moving along the steep mountain paths. If a cow would stop to eat an especially appetizing clump of grass, Rusty would start her moving again with a woof! Woof! The gentle cows would move along without complaint. After an hour or so, the cows, sheep, and horses would appear exiting the forest with Rusty trotting along behind with his tongue dangling from his mouth. He seemed so proud of himself. I always rewarded him with a pan of cool water, some hugs, and gentle pats upon his beautiful head.

One by one, I would move the cows into the milking stall. As I squeezed the cow's teats, streams of milk would make a pinging sound when striking the bottom of the large aluminum milk pails. As the pail began to fill, a foam would build up on the surface muting the sound of the squirting milk.

There were always from two to four large fat barn cats sitting patiently sitting side by side upon the wide wooden foundation sill at the bottom of the barn wall. I would aim a strong stream of milk from the cow's teat directly at their mouths. They would sit there licking the milk in mid air as it splattered all over their faces. It was a comical sight, but they seemed to enjoy it and they never failed to appear at milking time. Afterward, I gave them an ample supply of milk in a pan which I kept there for that purpose.

I am saddened to say that as years passed, Rusty and I were able to spend less and less time together. At the same time, our love of each other never diminished My elementary school was only a half mile from my home. Rusty would always walk to school with me and would return home alone to wait until school ended for the day at four o'clock. Be the weather hot or cold, sunny or rainy, winter or summer, Rusty would always be waiting for me at the exact same spot at the top of a low hill half way between the school and the farmhouse. He would wait until I was near fifty feet from him, when he would explode into a blur of flying feet and fur. At six feet away, he would leap into the air and crash into my chest. I would gather him into my arms and we would have a hug and tussle session. After a while, he would wiggle free and for the next several minutes he would yelp for joy. He would run big circles around me altering his course every few rounds in order to brush my legs as he zoomed past. He would finally fall flat upon his stomach exhausted as he awaited friendly pats on his head from his best Friend.

In the Fall of 1936, I began attending High School at Smoot, a village six miles from my home. School buses were not yet in use in the area in which I lived, so it was necessary for me to walk to Smoot each day, if I was to get an education. Rusty's and my routine did not change much during the summertime, and the only change during the school year was that I had to complete my chores earlier in the morning and later during the evening. Of course, Rusty could not accompany me the long trek to Smoot, but Rusty selected a spot in the road a half mile from the farmhouse where he waited for his Friend each evening. I always watched for him as he tried to be invisible by pressing his body as close to the ground as possible. He seemed to reason that he was taking me by surprise as he began his crushing charge. I always swung my book bag around to my back in preparation for the blast. The reunion was always the same. The intensity never diminished the four years that I attended Smoot High School.

I graduated just in time to be drafted into the Army during World War II. It was more than three years before I would be able to return home to see my dear Friend, Rusty. Letters from home informed me that he wasn't taking my absence well. He grieved and whimpered incessantly for many weeks and refused to eat for days at a time. He lost weight, became listless, and his fur became a grayish dull color. He would no longer drive the animals home from pasture. No more joyful romps. He just lay with his chin resting upon his outstretched paws and seemed to age ten years in just a few weeks. He could well imagine how I was also missing him.

The next time I saw Rusty was when I came home from the War. I was dropped off by a Greyhound bus driver at Sam Black Church, eight miles from our farm. I left my luggage with a friend at a near-by service station and set out walking for home. I climbed an old familiar path up the mountainside through the forest. The path had almost disappeared from disuse during the years that I had been gone. When I reached the edge of a large field at the top of the mountain, I shouted at the top of my lungs, "Here Rusty! Here Rusty!" I did not have long to wait. There came Rusty, not as fast as he used to run, but running as fast as his stiff legs could carry him, never-the-less. Gone was the bone-jarring impact of yesteryear, but the joy was still there. Rusty had aged. Gone was the beautiful coat of fur that I remembered. His brown eyebrows were gray and those deep lustrous brown pools that were his intelligent eyes were now dull cloudy blanks. His whiskers and the hairs around his nose were snow white. Rusty seemed that he could not get close enough to me as I sat upon the ground and hugged the dog tightly. Rusty whimpered softly as I rubbed my old Friend's head as my tears splashed down and wet the frizzy gray fur where they landed. We two Friends sat there with no concept of time until darkness settled over us.

I finally regained my composure. Rusty and I slowly walked the remaining four hundred yards to the farmhouse. I could see the glow of a kerosene lamp through the open kitchen door as I opened the creaky back gate a few feet from where Rusty was born. Rusty began to bark as the two old Friends reached the back porch as though he was shouting, "Hey everybody, Ed is home!"

James E. Martin

OUR ONE ROOM SCHOOL

In legend those schools were always painted red
But most were weathered gray instead
Bare clap-board sides on wooden frame
Icons of nostalgic country fame
The one room schools of yore
By bus replaced to be no more

Solidly built by carpenters' master hand
Efficient, yet of simple plan
Foundation strong, gabled roof of tin
Four two-sash windows to let light come in
Sturdy oak comprised the wooden floor
Access by only one entrance door

A belfry contained the school house bell
Whose clang class starting time would tell
That sound wafted across farm and glen
Announcing another school day would soon begin
From near and far came skipping feet
Through sunshine bright or snow and sleet

The little room was such a classic hall
Behind the Teacher's desk, the blackboard wall
Open faced bookcase in a nearby corner
Atop Teacher's desk lay disciplinary rod and pointer
Anchored to the floor four rows of desks and seats
A pot-bellied coal fired Burnside stove for heat

At the back of the room dangled the school bell rope

On the wall a row of nails upon which to hang our coats
Lard bucket lunch pails in a row atop a shelf
Inverted glass water jug on a steel frame stood by itself
Each Student took turns to get a sup
Of water from his personal collapsible aluminum cup

Our school was named for a family named Brown
It was located upon an acre of donated ground
There was also a coal house and two outside 'privies'
Many shade trees and playground for the kiddies
A board fence kept the little ones out of the road
Behind the school a field where a farmer using horses
    the hay he mowed

With first step from Mother's apron strings children came
Like small boats launched upon Life's uncertain main
To the care of Teacher's hand so firm
Capable of unconditional love or discipline stern
Haynes, Hutsenpiller, Frantz, Hedges to name a few
Were early school Masters whom I knew

School days lasted from nine o'clock till four
We learned Patriotism, our Homes and Country to adore
Along with Grammar, Geography, History, and Math
And to make our word our bond along Life's path
To respect our neighbors and to honor Law
And to live in harmony with one and all

Our ancient school has not lost its mystique
Oh! If those old walls could only speak!
Of children dressed in gingham and denim the would tell
And of boys dipping girls 'pigtails' into desktop ink wells

Of arithmetic matches and spelling bees
Games of hide and seek among the trees

Baseball games played using broomsticks for bats
Balls made of yarn unraveled from a knitted stocking cap
Games of fox and goose in Winter's snow
Farmer in the dell in Spring's warm glow
It was the Era of the Great Depression's grip so hard
There was no playground equipment in the yard

Those walls could recite all of the children's names
Kathryn, Mary, Wanda, J.L., Jim, Walter, Layton, and
    James
Myrtle, Margie, Marie, Calvin, Lacy, Jimmy, and Dale
Leroy, Louise, Lonzo, Larry, Lace, Lovena, Charles who
    married Gale
Ronald, Norman, Tommy, George, Biddy, Punny, Vivetta
Christine, Gladys, Loretta, Annetta, and Wanetta
Max, Jim, Herbert, Ardema. and Irmalee
And last of all - they would remember me

One cannot help but wonder where all have gone
Of course many have departed Life's final shore
It is sad they shall never again be as one
Rushing through that familiar open door
But in memory I imagine I hear that ringing bell,
    can see the shade so cool
The trees have grown much larger now, that surround
    Our beloved one room school

GENERAL JACK'S FIRST NIGHT OUT

The year was 1930. My Family lived two miles from the Crag Post Office in one direction and six miles from the Smoot Post Office in the opposite direction. The 'Great Depression' was tightening its grip to the point that my Father could no longer sell his timber products. The 'Great Dustbowl Drought' stunted crops in the fields adding more hardship to our survival. I spent nearly all of my summer days for two years drawing water from our well with a rope and bucket to pour into a washtub for our farm animals to drink.

One dollar per a ten-hour day of labor was considered good pay, if such demand for labor could be found. My Father desperately needed a job. An elderly man, who had carried the mail from Crag to Smoot on horseback for many years, notified the US Postal Department that he would not renew his contract in January, for, due to declining health, he could no longer endure exposure to West Virginia's severe winters on horseback. Father submitted the winning bid for the contract at thirty dollars per month working six-day weeks.

The greatest obstacle to delivering the mail on time were the enormous snow drifts of winter. West Virginia's winters are often severe, That was especially true during the decade of 1930. All roads in our Region were dirt, which were never good. The surface could turn from four inches of dust as fine textured as flour during dry weather to gooey mud during wet Weather. Farm wagons and the few

137

automobiles in the Area kept the roads engraved with hub-deep ruts throughout the years. Travelers were not confronted by only the cold of winter, but wind combined with heavy snowfall often filled the roadbeds with drifts a quarter mile long and more than six feet deep. Those conditions made foul weather travel almost impossible except by horseback. It was into this scene that this story took shape.

Father's joy of winning the mail contract was partially dulled by a problem that he had to face immediately. He needed fleet-footed horses that could make the two mile trip to Crag, the eight miles back past our farm to Smoot, the return to Crag, and the two miles back to our farm; a twenty mile round trip. The horses which he owned and used to provide power for the heavy farm work weighed eighteen hundred pounds each and were slow and powerful. It would require many hours at their plodding pace to cover twenty miles, besides it would not be fair to expect Ole Barney and Alex to work the farm and carry the mail too. Something had to be done quickly.

One of Father's brothers, who lived nearby, owned a fine small saddle-horse which he seldom rode. He loaned Father his horse until he could buy those he needed. It would not take many trips day after day carrying a two hundred pound man, a saddle, and a load of mail make a single horse sick and lame. At first, Father used one of the farm horses morning and afternoon to make the two mile trip to Crag and back, before transferring the mail to and from the saddle-horse. He needed a minimum of three long-legged fleet-footed animals to perform his duties and to allow sufficient rest to each.

I had another uncle who worked in a coal mine at Quinwood, a distance of approximately twenty miles from our farm. He told Father that most of the large mines in the area were installing electricity and would were replacing ponies and mules with electric motors to pull coal cars out of the mines. The mine animals were being sold at low prices. Uncle had seen a large powerful young mule named General Jack among the others. He was the largest mule Uncle had ever seen and that he had a reputation of being mean, stubborn, and unpredictable. Uncle believed that if General Jack could be broken to ride, he would be an ideal animal for carrying the mail.

Father made an arrangement with a neighbor who owned a car to take him to Quinwood one afternoon after completing the mail run for the day. He took a bridle with a snaffle bit and an Army saddle equipped with a pummel and double girth. Judging from what Uncle has told him about that mule, Father would need every advantage he could get.

The roads were in terrible condition following a sudden thaw of deep snow. The ruts were deep and filled with water making progress with that T-model Ford slow and difficult. It was late afternoon when the car finally chugged to a stop before the Quinwood Mine's business office. Fortunately for Father, General Jack was still available for purchase for twenty dollars. He made the purchase and released his friend to return home after taking Father to the mine's stable area.

The Stable Master assisted Father in mounting the first saddle Jack had ever seen upon his back. He did not take kindly to having himself being tightly bound around his middle by those two girths. He kicked and brayed his discontent which was a mild forecast of events to come when Father would attempt to ride him.

There was no time to waste, because night time was swiftly coming to one of the shortest days of the year and Father was going to be twenty miles from home with a renegade mule. The next day's seven o'clock mail pick-up was very much upon his mind. He could not be late and no one else could take his place.

There was only one hour of daylight remaining when the two men lead Jack out to the corral. Father asked the other man to pass a rope through the two rings on the bridle bit and to loop the ends around one of the fence posts. He further instructed the man to keep a firm hold on the rope until Father was seated in the saddle at which time he would signal for the rope to be released.

The trip from the stable to the corral had been turbulent with General Jack desperately kicking bucking, and braying with all of his lung power in attempts to free himself from that contraption squeezing the life out of him. It required the strength of both men just to hold onto the reins and lead him into the corral. The battle lines had been drawn and the mule was determined that strange man was not going to get upon his back. He lashed out at his tormentor with all four feet and exerted his best effort to dislodge the post out of the ground. Father was also young and powerful. With a swift move, he sprang into the saddle. With one hand gripping the pummel and the other grasping the reins, he signaled the Stable Master to release the rope.

The Stable Master had seen the determination in Father's eyes and he knew the reputation of that mule from the day when harness had first been placed upon his back. He positioned himself atop the corral fence prepared to observe what he thought would be the Super-bowl of bronk busting. As the show began, he was sure he would not be disappointed. If the two men had thought that General Jack exerted profound energy trying to free himself of the empty saddle, they now realized that was a mild imitation his antics now that he was free to move. He began making moves which had not been invented yet. Father had broken other animals to ride, but he had not ridden a buzz saw.

For openers, Jack was certain that he could get the man off his back by leaping high into the air, arching his back until his nose and all four feet touched each other, returning to earth with a fifteen hundred pound jolt, all four pivoting on one spot. When that didn't work, he emitted a groan that sounded as though it was originating inside a volcano and then bounded several short hops with his nose scraping the ground, zig zagged while wagging his head from side to side, and twisting his body in the shape of a quarter moon. He followed that by several high kicks that sent chunks of mud flying from his feet high into the air.

So far, the man doggedly hung on. Consumed by rage and frustration, the mule stood on his hind feet with his front feet pawing the air. He suddenly fell backward assuming the man would fall off and he could crush him. Farther simply stepped out of the way and allowed him to fall, springing upon the mule's back once more as the animal was in the act of regaining a standing position. Combat resumed with General Jack making an awesome high jump followed by several bone-jarring choppy leaps combined with swift alternating moves from side to side ending with an abrupt stop, arched back, nose to the ground high kick. Father lost control and went flying spread eagle through the air. He belly-whopped upon the muddy ground with a disgusting splat, scooting about eight feet before he stopped.

Score round one for General Jack!

The mule just stood where he had stopped, feet spread apart, head lowered, with the reins laying on the ground. His long hairy ears whose tips had been worn off from hundreds of hours being scraped against the mine's roof were now perked forward. He stared with hostility at the limping human mud-ball staggering hat in hand toward him. Father could dimly see the mule as he tried to clear the mud from his eyes by using the sleeve of his jacket. Jack didn't move a muscle as he stood there mockingly just as to say, "Come on big boy! Do you want to try again?"

Father gathered the reins once more and tried to remount, but General Jack was not in a cooperative mood. He simply side-stepped each attempt. After several unsuccessful tries, Father decided to move the mule alongside the corral fence where he could not move away.

That was when General Jack balked. True to the nature of mules the World over, he refused to move. That animal was filled with head to tail stubbornness. He sat down on his rump looking like a large stump covered by brown hair. Father tugged upon the reins, but that mule would not budge. He was wasting valuable time. Father had a sudden idea which possibly could get the mule to moving once more. He gathered a dead weed from the ground, grasped the reins beneath Jack's chin, and began tickling his nose with the weed. The mule resolutely resisted the weed to bother him, but, when Father changed tactics by inserting the weed into one of the mule's nostrils and began twisting it, Jack could no longer resist. He sprang to his feet with a snort, but Father did not quit; he let the weed remain inside the mule's nostril and took advantage of his confusion to back him into the fence. Father sprang into the saddle and the war was on once more.

Just as before, General Jack delivered a world-class performance. Father was determined that he would not be thrown again. He would just let the mule tire himself out. He dropped the reins over the pommel of the saddle and then held to it with both hands. Each time Jack's feet jolted the ground, Father felt a ringing sensation inside his ears and the pain inside his bruised body caused him to grunt. Jack showed no sign of weakening, so Father allowed him to go where ever he wished and simply held on.

The man seemed to be glued to his back, so Jack had a new idea. He made several short stiff-legged dashes as close to the fence as possible attempting to scrape the man off. Father saw through that strategy in time to lift his leg and avoid injury. The mule sensed that Father was thrown off balance, so once more he made a cat-like sideways move, stopped quickly, and kicked high. The maneuver worked and once more he sent Father crashing to the ground with a teeth-rattling thud!

Score round two for General Jack!

So the battle continued for an hour. General Jack had no idea of the nice home which Father was planning to give him. No more slaving inside that damp, dark, dangerous mine. Ahead lay green pastures, a comfortable stable, and good food, but for now, Jack was angry and covered by a foamy sweat. Father was never in doubt that he would finally win. When that time finally came, Jack was beaten, so what did he do? Yep, he sad down once more and refused to move.

Father's patience with that mule were exhausted. He could not get the twenty mile trip out of his mind and he dreaded th think about how bad he was going to feel at mail pick-up time in the morning. He knew that he needed to get that mule started homeward and soon. He had a fantastic idea that was certain to get that mule's attention. He placed a wad of chewing tobacco into his mouth and began chewing it, following which he marched up to General Jack, grasped one of his ears, and spat a generous squirt of tobacco juice into it!

Jack's response was somewhat akin to the lighting of a rocket! He bounded to his feet with bug-eyed dispair, dragging Father with his as he exploded into uncontrolled panic. He had never had any kind of substance inside an ear before. The roaring sensation caused by that liquid in his ear convinced his that something was about to take his head off! The snorting, flailing, and cavorting cleared most of the tobacco juice from his ear as he becalmed himself into a timid, trembling, defeated warrior. Father seized the opportunity to remount. He yelled for the Stable Master to open the gate and, at last, they were on their way home.

Darkness was settling in and the temperature had begun falling rapidly. The Pair created a strange sight as they emerged through the twilight into the dimly lighted streets of Quinwood. Both were covered with mud from head to foot. Father hardly resembled a man. That anyone would be riding a mule into the night in that remote mountain region did not make any logic to the people of the street. Most saw humor in the Pair's ridiculous appearance, but what amused them most was Father's obvious lack of control over that wild mule. General Jack had never been close to many people, so their shouting, laughing, and gesturing made him nervous. Also, being near cars and trucks for the first time made him insane! When dogs began chasing him, barking at his heels, he sucked his tail tightly between his hind legs, began galloping out of control weaving from one side of the street to the other as though he was riding some sort of crazy skate-board, and sending people on the sidewalks scurrying for safety. To say that both Father and General Jack were frightened would be an understatement; they were scared out of their wits. Father knew that he could not control the mule under those circumstances, but, at least, they were making forward progress as bystanders gleefully clapped their hands and yelled "Ride em cowboy!"

The travelers eventually reached the outskirts of town where only the squeaking of the saddle leather broke the silence. Jack walked quietly along the sodden roadbed. The four mile trip down the steep mountain road to Charmco was the only period of peace that either of the travelers had known since they first met during the late afternoon. Father spoke gently to the mule from time to time as they moved along. He occasionally patted the mule on a side of his neck to assure him that he really did want to be his friend. A fine drizzle borne upon a steady cold East wind began striking Father's face and freezing upon his mud-caked clothing, thus increasing misery to his bruised and aching body.

Upon reaching Charmco, the travelers encountered a new danger. That is where the Quinwood Mountain Road intersects US Route 60, the only paved two-lane highway in the Region. Motor vehicles were not plentiful during that Era and, due to the Depression, people could not afford to travel extensively. Furthermore, there was not much traffic at that time of evening.

Rainelle, at a distance of another four miles, was the next town through which Father and Jack must travel. Vehicles of the time did not travel at blurring speeds, but a vehicle moving at moderate speed was frightening to General Jack. For safety, Father would guide the mule into the side ditch when he heard a vehicle approaching from behind. With both being covered with mud combined with the fact that vehicular lights of the time were quite dim, it would be difficult for motorists to see them. As it were, most of those who did pass were not understanding of Father's problem. They could not comprehend why some fool would be riding a mule at that time of night during that kind of weather on a major highway. Some waited until alongside the Travelers, sounded their horns, and shouted, "Get off the road idiot."

After miserable hours, Rainelle town was behind them as Father and General Jack were moving along the dirt road that lead to the farm. General Jack was behaving himself and Father could not help thinking what a wonderful animal he was. There was almost a three hour trip ahead of them. Father was so hungry he was almost sick. He was shivering cold and, what was more, every part of his body ached from the beating that General Jack had given him. His clothing was now frozen almost as stiff as a suit of armor, and his nose and ears were numbed by the wind. As miserable as he was, he could not help wondering how the mule was feeling.

One by one they passed the farms and houses of people whom Father knew. Most of the houses were darkened for the night and the residents had gone to bed. On a few occasions, farm dogs came to the road to bark at the Travelers. Their presence disturbed Jack very much, although he was beginning not act as vigorously as he did to those encountered at Quinwood.

Four miles out of Rainell, they reached the lower foothills of Little Sewell Mountain where the farm is located.   Few houses along the road ahead where it meandered over steep grades, hollows, and dense forested mountains. A deep lonely feeling crept into Father as he daydreamed about home, supper, sleep, and the early morning ride he would be making to get the mail.   He allowed Jack to stop and rest periodically as he began to climb the steep mountain grades. He knew that the mule must be tired from the ordeal of the afternoon and the long trip. He knew, however, this experience was good training for breaking Jack into his forthcoming new way of life.

At a moment when they were approximately five hundred yards down the mountainside where Father's good friend Mr. Callison lived, he could not help smiling when he thought of the kindly old man with only one arm. He had lost the other in a coal mine accident. Over many years, he could not sleep well at night because of arthritis pains, so when his dogs barked at infrequent night-time travelers, the old man had a reputation of swinging a kerosene lantern over his front yard fence to see who was passing by. Drivers whose cars became stalled in the mud or snow on that terrible hill, were grateful when Mr. Callison employed his team of horses to tow them to the top of the grade. Father was wondering if he would be seeing his old Friend and his light this night.

Father was due t know the answer to that question much sooner than he anticipated. Daydreams disappeared with a blur of action! General Jack was moving quietly along one edge of the road avoiding hub-deep ruts when one of his feet bumped into a rabbit which had bedded down for the night in a pile of leaves. The rabbit exploded into a burst of speed! That was all it required to send Jack into hair-raising terror. The swiftness with which the mule moved sideways across the road made Father's head swim! Jack attempted to turn back to the direction from which they came, but he tripped over the deep ruts and sprawled head-first into the bank on the opposite side of the road, Father was unbalanced by the sudden move and was sent crashing to the ground taking the bridle with him. Fortunately for Father, Jack resumed climbing the hill, galloping toward Mr. Callison's house.

Dazed, muddied, and bloodied, Father wearily rose to his to his feet. He did not search or his hat, which was lost somewhere in the darkness. He attempted to run up the slippery road, agonizing over the knowledge that a wild mule was now loose in dozens of square miles of rugged uninhabited mountain forestland and that he may never be able to capture his again. He began shouting as loud as he could, hoping that Mr. Callison's dogs would hear him and alert the old man with the lantern. One thing was in Father's favor; Mr. Callison had lined both sides of the road with split-rail fences.

Father was yelling, "Hey Jim! Hey Jim!" Suddenly, he saw the lantern appearing in the distance. In his mind he said, "Thank God!" Now he only hoped that the mule had not passed Jim's house before the old man reached the road and held his lantern above his gate.

Lanterns were something which General Jack understood. He had seen them used hundreds of times inside the mine. If someone was swinging one of them back and forth, that meant Stop! For him, the dogs were another problem. He was dead tired from the rigors of that most unusual day, his most recent gallop up that steep hill not-with-standing. If the dogs wanted to eat him, come on. His resistance was gone. He took refuge in one of the fence corners where he was not going to tempt Fate any longer. When Father arrived panting and puffing, the gentle Mr. Callison had quieted his dogs and was holding the trembling mule around its neck with his only arm.

My grateful Father was embarrassed to say the least, but his Friend Jim was hungry for an explanation of why a sane man would be out past mid-night in the dead of winter riding a dad-burned lop-eared mule!

Well, my Father felt that a man who had just done him an immense favor certainly deserved a detailed explanation, so he obliged. Mr. Callison complimented him upon purchasing such a magnificent animal and surmised that he would prove to be a great asset if Father didn't kill him first before getting him home. Father said that he didn't have any quarrel with that. He thanked his Friend for his help and surmised that he had better move on. He was still at least three miles from home in an area where there were no more houses where he could get help if more trouble happened. He decided to reduce the chances of that by leading the mule the remaining distance home. If there were going to be any more surprises, he could at least hold to the reins.

As it happened, there were no more surprises. The farm was a welcome sight as Father opened the barnyard gate and led General Jack through the barn door into his nice warm stall. Jack was greeted by the gentle nickers of the three horses. Father filled his manger with hay and fed him a mixture of oats and shelled corn. He waited until Jack finished eating the grain after which he fetched him a bucket of clean water.

The time was near one o'clock AM before Father entered the house where Mother, who had no means with which to communicate with him during his long absence, awaited him almost sick with worry. He had removed his mud and ice caked clothing on the back proch before entering the house. He washed his face and hands before eating supper. Following that, he shampooed and bathed, before collapsing into bed. The last words he said to Mother before falling to sleep were, "This has been a mighty long day."

PATHS

Have you ever wondered who made the path upon which
    you walk today
What ancient time, what task at hand
Caused someone to pass that way
To leave his mark upon the land
For future feet to tread
Aware of only the Past he has known
Not knowing what yet may lie ahead

Some paths are straight and narrow, others wide and easy
Comfort is knowing that they are always there
As you ponder their long history
The trail may wind around the bend, of its end the view
    unclear
O'er hills obscured past forests, fields, and streams
A stroll through time when others sought fulfillment of their
    Dreams

Life, too, is like a path you walk as recently as today
For good or bad, up hill or down
You alone must chart your way
Straight to your Goal or meander in search of Opportunity's
    open door
Until you discover the thread tying Eternity to some ancient
    Lore
It may be the Path, the well-worn Path
Where millions have walked before

Paths it is true lead both ways
The Journey's lessons learned
You have watched the Sun-set die, when Morning comes, it
    will return
The Mileposts of years tell how far you have come
But Life goes on and its end for you untried, you roam
And the familiar Path which has brought you thus far
Can also lead you Home

JAMES E. MARTIN